CLAUS FOR CELEBRATION

ANNABELLE ARCHER WEDDING PLANNER
MYSTERY #15

LAURA DURHAM

BROADMOOR BOOKS

For Cathy Jaquette,
the OC and an amazing friend

CHAPTER 1

"I think we've made a huge mistake, Annabelle," my assistant, Kate, said as she walked into my apartment carrying several canvas tote bags slung over her shoulders. She dropped them on the floor, kicked off her high heels, and collapsed onto my couch.

"You couldn't find the ice-blue paper?" I asked, bending over and pawing through the bags with one hand while holding my bottled Mocha Frappuccino with the other.

"Oh, I found it." She flicked a hand through her blond bob. "Along with the ball ornaments and the 'naughty' and 'nice' signs for the drinks." She cast her eyes around my apartment, lingering on the sparsely decorated Christmas tree in the corner. "Good thing, too. This place needs a little oomph. I thought Richard was helping with party decor. Unless he's going through a minimalist phase again."

"He got delayed yesterday. Some important meeting that's going to change all of our lives." I padded back to the kitchen in my bare feet, taking a swig of my cold, sweet drink as I walked. I resumed buttering the toast I'd left on the counter when Kate had walked in, and I now peered at her across the opening between my kitchen and living room. "So what's this huge mistake we're making?"

"Taking on all this work. We usually slow down in December. All of our corporate planner friends get crazy and our hotel contacts are too busy to eat, but the holidays are usually the one time of the year when we can catch our breath." She motioned to the bags strewn across my floor. "Where's my break?"

I took a bite of toast, savoring the Irish butter my fiancé had gotten me hooked on, and chased it with a gulp of cold mocha-flavored coffee. Kate was right. December was usually downtime for wedding planners. Only the most stalwart brides wanted to compete with corporate holiday parties for event space or pay the holiday premiums. As the owner of Wedding Belles, Washington DC's most on-the-rise wedding planning company, I usually blocked off the month for rest and regrouping and catching up on sleep after the busy autumn and before the intense booking season that started in January. This year, however, my usual plan had flown out the window.

Carrying my plate of toast and drink out with me to the living room, I sat down next to Kate on the couch. "I know this month has been unusual, but might I remind you that the engagement party was your idea?"

She sat up and tilted her head at me. "Because we haven't had a free weekend all fall. If we don't have it now, you and Hottie Cop will never have a proper party to celebrate your engagement. I know you like to put off anything personal, but since you put me in charge of your wedding planning, we're throwing you and Reese a party." She flopped back again. "I just didn't know we'd have to work it around two weddings, including one on New Year's Eve."

"Neither did I," I said, holding out the plate and offering her a piece of toast, which she waved away. "Who knew we'd get a last-minute New Year's Eve wedding?"

"Don't get me wrong. The extra money will be nice, especially since they're paying our holiday wedding premium, but you know what a sacrifice it is for me to work on New Year's Eve, Annabelle."

I did know. As a champion dater, New Year's Eve was typically one of her busiest nights of the year. Kate had been known to fit in multiple dates on New Year's Eve, flitting between fancy restaurant seatings and over-the-top parties. Personally, I didn't know how she juggled it all, since I was more of the type to ring in the new year on my couch in my PJs.

"I promise I'll make it up to you," I said. "If anyone books a last-minute Valentine's Day wedding, I'll do it solo. And aside from lots of new meetings with potential clients, January and February are dead."

She gave me a side-eye glance. "I suppose I can survive until then. Fern is working on a new system to streamline my Valentine's dates this year, so hopefully it won't be as much of a disaster as last year."

I remembered the year before had involved wireless headsets, spreadsheets, and plenty of hysterics on our hairdresser friend Fern's part.

"I thought I remembered something about you wanting to slow down your dating pace and find someone to get serious with." I tucked my feet up under me. "What happened to that?"

She draped one arm across the back of the yellow twill couch cushions, drumming her pink, polished fingernails on the fabric. "There is one guy I could see myself with, but I'm not sure if I'm ready to settle down yet."

"The lawyer from Williams & Connolly?" I asked.

She shook her head.

"The guy who works at the White House?"

She wrinkled her nose. "No one dates White House staffers anymore. Anyway, I'm not into young guys who work on the Hill anymore. This guy's more . . .established."

Established? I knew what that was a code word for. I tried to remember her mentioning an older guy, but I'd always found it hard to keep track of her men. "Did you finally decide to get a sugar daddy?"

Kate gave me a scandalized look. "He's not *that* old, besides, I gave up that idea when Wedding Belles took off, and you raised my salary." She darted her eyes to me. "He's not your typical DC guy. He's older and not involved in politics or the government at all. Plus, he's completely different from me in almost every way."

I shrugged. "You know what they say. Opposites attract."

"Speaking of opposites." Kate craned her neck toward the hallway of my apartment. "Where is your very attractive opposite?"

"Reese?" I asked, glancing down the hall, even though I knew my fiancé wasn't there. "He went into the precinct early this morning.

There's been an uptick in shoplifting and pickpocketing around Georgetown, and one of their prime suspects showed up outside the station tied up in gold Christmas garland with a bow around his mouth."

Mike Reese was not only my fiancé, he was a DC police detective I'd met when one of our clients had been murdered at a wedding. It had taken us a few years--and a few more dead bodies--before we'd started dating, but we'd been living together for almost a year and had been engaged for several months.

"So he was literally gift wrapped for them?" She flipped a hand through her hair. "Which proves that the city is crazy at the holidays, which is why we don't take weddings in December, which is why it's insane that we have a wedding at the Four Seasons on Saturday and your engagement party on Sunday, not to mention the last-minute planning for the New Year's wedding."

She gasped for breath.

"We can handle it." I took a final bite of now-cold toast and drained the Frappuccino, standing and heading for the kitchen with the empty plate and bottle. "It isn't like we've never had two events on a weekend."

"Yes." Kate stood and walked to the opening between the two rooms, leaning over the counter and poking her head into the kitchen. "But how wrecked have we looked the second day? I refuse to let you go to your own engagement party looking like you did at the Turner-Finley wedding."

I dropped the empty bottle in my recycling bin. "How did I look at that wedding?"

She waved a hand in my general direction. "Like this. Hair in a ponytail. Hardly any makeup. Like you don't care."

I touched a hand to my bare face and glanced down at the jeans and T-shirt I'd thrown on. "I *don't* care. It's barely ten in the morning, and we don't have a meeting until this afternoon. This morning is supposed to be about finalizing all the vendors for Saturday and putting together gift bags."

"Fine," she said. "But I hope you're planning on a cute outfit to go see Buster and Mack later. It's one of the few in-person meetings we're going to have with our New Year's bride before the wedding day."

I made a mental rundown of my closet and the size of my dry-cleaning bag. "Don't worry. I've got plenty of cute winter outfits."

Kate made a face. "You might want to rethink that." She cut her eyes to her own short black skirt and white button-down opened low at the neck. "Why do you think I'm not wearing a coat in December?"

I'd assumed it was so she could show as much leg and cleavage as possible. "What are you talking about?"

Kate made tsk-ing noises at me. "You never check the weather, do you? We got a warm snap. It's seventy-eight degrees outside and will be all week."

"In December?" I gaped at her. "But Saturday's wedding is snowflake themed. Everything is icicles and ice blue. We have an outside s'mores station and hot chocolate bar."

"Yeah, that's going to be a little weird."

I slumped against the kitchen counter, hearing my office phone ringing down the hall. If I was a betting woman, I'd have put money on that being Saturday's bride calling in a panic because her wintry wedding was now going to be pleasantly warm instead of cool and cozy. I knew I'd have to work some serious wedding planner Zen magic to convince her that her day wouldn't be a disaster. Even though I told all my brides the only thing I couldn't control was the weather, they still seemed to think I could whip out a mythical cure-all when it poured rain or when temperatures soared to near one hundred degrees in the summer.

The door flew open, and my best friend, Richard Gerard, staggered into my apartment, dropping a plastic crate on the floor with a loud thud. His gaze went from the scantily decorated Christmas tree to me, and he let out a tortured sigh.

"The next time I have another brilliant idea like this, will someone please shoot me?"

Kate grinned at me. "Dibs."

CHAPTER 2

"Neither this absurd warm weather nor you living on the
fourth floor of a walk-up is getting me in the holiday spirit,"
Richard said as he fanned himself with two hands. "Thank
heavens I didn't wear my cashmere. Much more of this, and I'm going
to need to pull my summer wardrobe back out. Trust me when I say I
do not have time to air out my linen suits right now."

He swung his black leather man bag off his shoulder and set it on
the ground. As it tipped over, a tiny black-and-brown Yorkie popped
out of the top and scampered out, yipping happily as he ran around
sniffing.

"Poor Hermès can't even wear his sweaters," Richard said, fluttering a hand at the small dog. "What's the point of having Gucci if
you can't wear it?"

"One of the great questions of the universe," Kate said under her
breath as she scratched Hermès under the chin.

"Don't worry," I said, joining Richard in the living room as he
brushed off the sleeves of his royal blue blazer with a lint brush that
seemed to have materialized out of thin air. "I was just explaining to
Kate that the week might be a little packed, but it's nothing we can't
handle. We've all had multiple events on a weekend before."

"Indeed," he said absently, his gaze scouring my apartment while he frowned.

As the owner of Richard Gerard Catering, one of the premier catering companies in the area, Richard was adept at juggling parties. I knew back-to-back events were not enough to send him over the edge, although he did live most of his life close to it. Or, as Kate liked to put it, on the brink of insanity.

"Is it the rehearsal dinner or my engagement party that has you worried?" I asked. "Or are you still peeved the couple decided on a hotel for their actual wedding reception, because you know I can't force them to choose an off-premise venue. You did get their rehearsal dinner, and it's a pretty elaborate one."

"What?" He shook his head. "Of course not. I got over that ages ago."

I didn't point out that he'd been complaining about it only two days prior. I'd found with Richard it was better not to have a perfect memory.

I rested a hand on his sleeve. "I promise you it will all be fine. Tell him our new Wedding Belles motto, Kate."

"It's handled," Kate said, spreading her hands out in front of her as if she were unfurling a sign. "We're thinking of putting it on T-shirts."

I looked down at the crate at his feet. "We can set out the holiday decor you brought, and we'll be halfway to having this place decorated for the engagement party."

"About that," Richard said, not meeting my eyes. "I may have added a teensy little 'to-do' to your week."

"How teensy?" Kate asked, both hands on her hips as she eyed him.

"Don't be upset, Annabelle." He shifted from one foot to the other. "But I may have arranged for a photographer from *DC Life Magazine* to do a profile piece on Wedding Belles."

"Why would that make me upset?" I asked. "We've been dying to get into that magazine. A profile on our business would be huge."

He bent over his plastic crate and began pulling out holiday decor. "I'm glad you're pleased, darling. Now all we need to do is get your apartment in shape for the magazine's photo shoot."

My stomach tightened as I glanced around the slightly unkempt and severely unstyled living room. Client files were strewn across one end of the dining room table, and one of Reese's jackets was hooked over the back of a chair. Wedding magazines sat stacked high in a rack by the couch, and my glass coffee table held nothing but more paperwork and an unwashed coffee mug. "A photo shoot? In my apartment?"

"I tried to convince them to do it somewhere else." He sighed deeply as he scanned the space. "But they insist on capturing their subjects in their homes and offices. They want a real behind-the-scenes look."

I groaned. Unfortunately for me, my apartment also doubled as Wedding Belles headquarters, with the home office down the hall housing filing cabinets, a rarely-used desk, and a vast assortment of leftover wedding favors, gift bags, and programs. Despite planning over-the-top weddings for clients, my own design style was decidedly simplistic. I usually argued that I didn't have time to keep my life and my clients' weddings styled, but the truth was I wasn't a fussy person when it came to myself. I favored yoga pants and jeans over cute dresses, and would rather have a comfortable home than a fussy one. I was a substance over style woman, and I knew that did not lend itself to stunning photos.

Kate flopped back onto the couch, and Hermès immediately jumped up and began licking the hand draped over her head. "We're doomed."

"Nonsense," Richard said, adopting the take-charge tone he used when addressing his waiters or his dog. Accordingly, Hermès froze, his eyes on Richard. "All this place needs is a thorough cleaning, all new furniture, a fresh coat of paint, and some sort of design aesthetic."

"Oh, is that all?" Kate asked, propping herself up on her elbows. "And this is in between final preparations for this weekend's wedding, planning for our New Year's Eve wedding, and pulling together Annabelle's engagement party?"

Richard swiveled his head toward me, and his dark spiky hair didn't so much as quiver. "A New Year's Eve wedding? When were you going to mention this to me?"

"That's what you took away from all of that?" I asked.

He sniffed, looking slightly abashed. "Fine. Perhaps this isn't the best time to have a photography team descend on your apartment, but when opportunity knocks, Annabelle, you have to open the door."

"Yoo hoo!" A head popped around the front door that Richard had left standing open.

"And when you come *here*, you have to remember to close the door," I muttered to Richard as my downstairs neighbor Leatrice bustled inside wearing a reindeer sweater with three-dimensional googly eyes, her jet-black hair adorned with a blinking reindeer antler headband. "And lock it."

"I thought I heard barking," she said, making a beeline for Hermès.

For a woman who had cruised past her eightieth birthday, she had remarkably acute hearing. She also considered herself an amateur spy, so she possessed an apartment full of listening devices. It was anyone's guess which she'd employed today.

"What's up, Leatrice?" I asked. "We're kind of in the middle of a crisis here."

Her eyebrows popped up, and she pursed her bright-coral lips. "Another murder?"

"No," I said with a sigh. "It's not like we stumble over dead bodies every day."

"It's been months since we had anything to do with a murder investigation," Kate added, counting quickly on her fingers. "Over eight months. I think that's a record for us."

"You aren't counting the body you found on my wedding day?" Leatrice asked as she rubbed Hermès's belly.

Kate shook her head. "He wasn't dead. I'm only counting actual corpses."

"I think I know who you *shouldn't* have at the magazine interview," Richard said out of the corner of his mouth.

"As much fun as this is," I said, giving my assistant a pointed look, "we really need to get to work if we're going to get everything done before the weekend."

"That's why I popped by, dear," Leatrice said. "My honeybun

wanted to see if you needed anything for your engagement party in the way of performers."

Leatrice had recently married Sidney Allen, an entertainment coordinator who provided costumed performers for events. The two had met when Leatrice crashed a Venetian-themed wedding I'd planned that had been filled with Carnival characters courtesy of Sidney Allen.

"Performers?" Richard sucked in a breath. "What type of performers does 'honeybun' suggest for an engagement party?"

"It is two weeks before Christmas," Leatrice said. "We thought elves could be fun."

"Elves?" Kate cocked her head to one side. "Like the hot Orlando Bloom, *Lord of the Rings* kind or the short jingle-bell hat, Santa Claus kind?"

Leatrice giggled. "The Santa Claus kind, of course."

"Oh, no." Richard held up his hands, palms out. "Just because this party is taking place in December does not mean we're going to have an apartment full of little people in pointy shoes running around."

"Sidney Allen doesn't actually use little people for his elves, does he?" I asked. "I feel like that isn't very PC."

Leatrice nibbled the corner of her bottom lip. "I'm not sure. They might not be little people. They might be children."

"Child labor," Richard mumbled. "Even better."

"I don't think we need any elves," I said to Leatrice, "but please tell Sidney Allen that we appreciate the offer."

"The party's pretty set," Kate added. "Food by Richard, décor by Buster and Mack. Annabelle doesn't want a fuss."

My elderly neighbor shrugged. "Probably for the best. My poor sugar muffin is stretched pretty thin with all the Santas he's providing for holiday parties. But don't worry. I can still bring my pigs-in-a-blanket wreath."

Richard clutched my arm for support, and I hoped he wasn't going into a full-on swoon.

"I think we're set on food, too," I said. "Richard's doing the catering, and you know his rules about outside food."

The official rule was that he preferred outside food not be brought to events he catered because he was responsible for the food safety of the party. The reality was that he would toss it out a window.

"Too bad," Kate said. "I love a good pig-in-a-blanket. Especially when said pigs are arranged to look like a Christmas wreath."

Richard shot her a look, but before he could say something, the door swung open.

Fern, hairdresser to the rich and famous of DC and our go-to wedding hairstylist, staggered into the room. His dark hair was pulled back into a low ponytail, and he wore cranberry-colored pants and a dark-gray turtleneck. A few strands of hair fell in his face as he leaned against the armrest of my couch. "Thank goodness you're all here."

"What's wrong?" I asked. Fern was always impeccably put together, rarely a hair out of place.

"It's Santa Claus," he said, pressing a hand to his throat. "He's missing."

CHAPTER 3

"Have I been sucked into an alternate universe?" Richard asked, looking from face to face. "Santa can't be missing because . . ." He darted a glance at Hermès. "Well, I don't want to say it out loud."

Kate put her hands over the small dog's pointy ears. "Because he's not real?"

"Not the *real* Santa Claus," Fern said. "Kris Kringle Jingle. The man who dresses up in a Santa costume and walks around Georgetown singing holiday songs to people."

Leatrice clapped her hands together. "Oh, I love him. He always compliments me on my hair and does the best version of 'Jingle Bell Rock.'" Her face fell. "Did you say he's missing?"

Fern nodded, dropping into the overstuffed yellow twill chair positioned across from my couch. "At least according to my friend, Jeannie."

I headed toward the kitchen to get Fern some water, since his cheeks were flushed pink. I snagged a bottle from the fridge and leaned my head over the divider between the rooms. "How does Jeannie know he's missing and not just taking some time off? I'm sure wearing a Santa costume when it's almost eighty degrees isn't fun."

"Jeannie knows everything that goes on in Georgetown," Fern said, fanning himself with a linen handkerchief, his head tipped back against the cushion. "If she thinks he's missing, then he's missing."

I returned to the living room and handed Fern the bottled water, then perched on the arm of the couch, resigning myself to the fact that nothing was going to get done until Fern finished his story.

He winked at me. "You're an angel, Annabelle."

"Is this Jeannie someone you work with?" Kate asked. "Have you taken on a new stylist in the salon?"

Fern took a long drink of water, then laughed. "Aren't you a stitch? No, Jeannie is one of the housing challenged of Georgetown."

"Housing challenged?" Richard tilted his head. "Do you mean homeless?"

"Yes, but it's not like she lives on the streets. She moves from shelter to shelter," Fern said. "We met when she was sitting outside the salon one day, and I offered to give her a wash and dry. Now she comes in just about every week. And she's the one I save all my hotel toiletries for. Jeannie loves the little bottles."

"How often do you stay in hotels?" Kate asked.

Fern smoothed a loose strand of hair back into his ponytail. "I'm in hotels almost every weekend. I may not *stay* there per se."

"Are you telling me you take the toiletries out of the hotel rooms where our brides are getting ready?" I asked, caught between feeling scandalized and impressed.

He gave a half shrug. "Maybe. Trust me when I tell you that Jeannie gets more enjoyment out of them than anyone could."

Richard gave an impatient sigh. "So how did this street person decide that the singing Santa is missing?"

"Like I said," Fern gave Richard an equally impatient look. "She knows everything that goes on in Georgetown. She's the one who told me that Violet Drummond was having an affair with a diplomatic intern thirty years younger than her."

Richard's eyebrows shot up, but I jumped in before he and Fern could go down the rabbit hole of society gossip they both adored. "So how long does Jeannie say he's been missing?"

"At least a day." Fern sat up. "She claims that Kris Kringle Jingle told her he was nervous about something he'd seen the day before yesterday. He wouldn't go into more detail, but claimed he saw something he shouldn't have, and he hoped *they* hadn't seen him."

Leatrice's eyes were as round as the googly reindeer eyes on her sweater. "Hope who hadn't seen him?"

"That's what she doesn't know," Fern said. "But Jeannie hasn't seen him since then, and she's convinced something bad has happened to him."

"It does sound suspicious."

We all swung our heads toward the deep voice and the doorway where my fiancé, Mike Reese, stood listening.

I jumped up, my heart fluttering a bit seeing him. Even though we now lived together, I still got butterflies each time I saw my tall fiancé with dark hair and hazel eyes. "I didn't know you'd be home so early."

He scanned the crowd in our apartment, one eyebrow lifting slightly. He'd gotten used to my colorful friends coming in and out of our place—mostly work-related, since Wedding Belles operated out of our Georgetown apartment—but it wasn't every day so many of them were camped out in the living room.

Leatrice leapt to her feet, jostling Hermès, who gave a disapproving yip, and she rushed over to Reese. "It seems like we've stumbled into another mystery, Detective."

"No." I waved a finger. "No, we haven't. There's no mystery." The last thing I needed to add to my already jam-packed schedule was a criminal investigation. I knew from past experience that our investigations usually took over everything, and I could not afford the distraction this week.

Reese grinned at me. "I'm glad to hear you saying that. I don't know if I've ever heard you insist there *isn't* a case."

I resisted the urge to make a face at him. "There's a first time for everything. Besides, Richard just told me he arranged to have a Wedding Belles magazine shoot in our apartment this week on top of the wedding we have to pull together for Saturday and the party we're supposedly hosting on Sunday."

Reese ran a hand through his hair, and an errant curl flopped down on his forehead. "Maybe I should plan to clear out until next week."

"Don't you dare," I said, walking over and slipping my hand into his. "You're the only thing that's going to keep me sane."

He smiled and pulled me close to him. "We definitely don't want you going insane."

"So what do I tell Jeannie?" Fern asked, tapping one toe on the floor. "That it's bad timing for her friend to go missing?"

"You have to admit," Kate said, "two weeks before Christmas is not the time to get anyone's attention."

"Who is the missing person?" Reese asked.

"Kris Kringle Jingle," Fern said.

Leatrice bounced up and down on her toes. "You know. The fellow who dresses as Santa and walks around singing holiday songs in Georgetown."

A look of recognition flashed across my fiancé's face. "I do know him. He's been doing that for years. We keep him on our radar--like we keep any street performer--but he's never gotten any complaints. How long has he been missing?"

Fern stood. "At least twenty-four hours. Possibly more. My friend Jeannie can tell you more."

Reese nodded, then looked down at me. "Why don't I go talk with this Jeannie? That way you don't have to get sucked into an investigation, and I can file an official police report if we need to."

"You mean do things the official way?" Kate tapped a finger on her chin. "No hiding bodies or searching for evidence behind the backs of the police? Now that's a novel approach."

I ignored her comment and stared up at my handsome fiancé. "You sure you have the time?"

He kissed me on the forehead. "I'm sure, as long as it will keep you from running around trying to solve the case on your own. I'm on my lunch break, anyway. I'll just grab something quick while Fern and I are out."

"Lunch break?" I glanced up at the clock on my wall, preparing to tease him about taking such an early lunch, but swallowing hard when I saw the time. "It's after eleven already? Ugh! We have a floral meeting soon, and I'm not dressed."

Reese gave me a quick kiss and stepped back. "I'd better leave you to it, babe. I'll see you tonight." He beckoned Fern. "You're with me."

Fern trilled his fingers together as he followed Reese out the door, turning to wave at us. "This is so exciting. An official police investigation."

The butterflies in my stomach that my fiancé had produced had morphed into a tight ball. I hadn't gotten any of the confirmation calls made for Saturday's wedding, and I could only hope that the meeting with Buster and Mack would be quick.

Kate stood and steered me toward the hallway. "You get dressed while Richard and I talk about the photo shoot and the party."

"And why don't I take Hermès downstairs with me while you kids work?" Leatrice asked. "It's been ages since I babysat."

Richard's gaze went between his little dog and his crate of decor. "Fine, but no elf caps on him."

Leatrice's smile drooped, but she made a criss cross over her heart as she scooped up the Yorkie and headed out of my apartment. "You have my word."

I thought there was a much greater chance she had a matching set of reindeer antlers for him, but I didn't say anything as I hurried down the hall to get dressed. My mind went to the potentially missing Santa, then I shook my head. I'd been honest when I'd told Reese that the last thing I needed was to get pulled into another investigation, but I also felt a pang of guilt when I thought about Kris Kringle Jingle.

Just like everyone who lived in Georgetown, I'd grown used to the cheery sight of the slightly rumpled Santa who sang merrily as he strolled up and down M Street. He was as much a part of the neighborhood as the C&O Canal that cut through it and the colorful row houses lining the narrow streets. I forced myself not to think the worst as I pulled off my jeans and pawed through my dry-cleaning bag.

First a heat wave and now a missing Santa? The holidays weren't off to a great start.

CHAPTER 4

"That's not half bad for something you grabbed from the floor," Kate said as she appraised my black pants and hunter green top while holding open the door to Buster and Mack's flower shop.

The bell overhead tinkled as we walked inside Lush, and we were greeted by the store's familiar aroma of cut flowers and espresso, now mixed with the sharp scent of evergreen.

"I didn't grab it from the floor." I tried to sound indignant, even though, to be fair, the pants had been rescued from my dry-cleaning bag.

She plucked a strand of carpet lint from my pant leg. "I stand corrected."

"Fine," I said, under my breath, even though I didn't see any customers milling about the display tables that were stacked tall with holiday candles, glittering ornaments, and frosted-glass vases. "I may have gotten a little behind on laundry."

Kate held up her hands. "No judgment. I told you we needed some downtime. December is supposed to be the month where we get all our wedding day dresses cleaned and mended."

I sighed, knowing she was right. My dry-cleaning bag was jammed with black dresses, and my favorite black flats were in desperate need of a little love and a lot of shoe polish.

We stepped further inside and started to weave our way around the displays. Lush was usually what I would have called industrial chic, with concrete floors and metal shelves filled with galvanized buckets of fresh flowers lining the walls. Since November, however, it had transformed into a winter wonderland with a towering frosted Christmas tree in each corner, and the buckets of hydrangea and roses replaced with white birch branches and crimson amaryllis.

"Annabelle! Kate!" Mack appeared from the back of the shop, waving with one large hand and holding a tiny espresso cup with the other. "Make sure you pull the door closed tightly. I don't want the heat to wilt all of our evergreens."

As he lumbered toward us, I was reminded how incongruous a burly, leather-clad biker with a dark-red goatee, tattoos, and piercings was in a floral shop decked out with Christmas trees glistening with fake snow, pine wreaths hanging from velvet ribbon, and white twinkle lights dripping like icicles from the ceiling. When he reached us, I realized he wore a baby carrier strapped to his back, and a small, fair head poked around the side of his.

"Hey, Mack." I stood up on tiptoes to give him a kiss on the cheek, and then reached out for the child's chubby fist. "And hi, Merry."

"She's gotten so big," Kate said as the child unleashed a torrent of happy chatter and clapped her hands.

"Well, she is a year old," Mack reminded us, twisting his head and catching the little girl's eye.

"I can't believe it." Kate shook her head as Mack led us to the back of the shop and a long, high metal table surrounded by tall barstools. "Has it really been a year already?"

I thought back to the same time last year when Buster and Mack had found Merry on the doorstep of their biker church. A lot had happened since then, including Merry and her teenaged mother coming to live above Lush, and Buster and Mack becoming surrogate fathers to both of them. I looked at the chubby legs dangling from the metal frame carrier hooked on Mack's back. Only a few months ago, Merry was traveling in a front-facing fabric carrier, and now the little girl with blond hair curling around her ears looked almost ready to walk.

"We were going to do a big birthday party," Mack said, downing the last of his espresso. "But you know how crazy December is for florists. Between the home installations and the holiday parties, we're stretched thin."

"And this year it's also crazy for wedding planners." Kate hopped onto one of the barstools and set her pink purse beside her.

"You two don't normally have more than one wedding over the holidays, do you?" Mack asked, waving a hand toward the elaborate, chrome espresso machine behind him. "Cappuccino? Espresso?"

"No, we don't, to the question about holiday weddings," Kate said, "and yes, please, to the cappuccino. I need all the caffeine I can get."

"Make that two," I said, taking a seat as Mack bustled around the machine, Merry bobbing behind him.

"Now which wedding are we meeting about today?" Mack asked, then swiveled his head around quickly. "Son of a nutcracker! It's not the bride for this Saturday, is it? I've already placed her floral order."

"No," I assured him. "We're all set for that one. This is for the New Year's Eve wedding."

"Thank heavens." He glanced toward the ceiling, and I suspected he was saying a small prayer of thanks. Aside from being the city's top event florists, Buster and Mack were also members of a Christian motorcycle gang and the Born Again Biker Church. They'd reformed their previous lives, and now they never drank, cursed, or took the Lord's name in vain. It also appeared that their creative alternatives to cursing were seasonally inspired.

"Don't get too happy," Kate told him, raising her voice to be heard above the screeching of the espresso machine's steaming wand. "We only booked the wedding recently, and we know almost nothing about it."

"Except that they fired their old planner and are throwing out whatever work she'd done for them." I shifted on the barstool and put the client's thin file on the table in front of me. "The bride isn't even joining us today. She just called us to say something came up and to go ahead without her."

Mack looked over his shoulder. "Do we have creative carte blanche?"

"As long as you stick with the theme of 'time'," I said. "And the couple wants an Old World feel."

"So that's a no," Mack said, then shrugged. "That's fine. I'd rather have some direction than none at all."

I opened the file and stared down at the notes I'd taken when I'd talked to the bride on the phone. "Aside from keeping the venue and photographer and basic theme, we're starting from zero. I'd hoped to get the old floral proposals this morning so you could see what the client doesn't want, but we got a little derailed."

"By Santa Claus," Kate added.

Mack placed two oversized cappuccinos in front of us, then turned back to the machine to retrieve his own refilled demitasse cup. "Now this I want to hear."

"It's nothing really." I wrapped my hands around the warm cup and enjoyed the heat, even if it wasn't cold outside. "Fern is all worked up because a friend of his claims that Kris Kringle Jingle is missing."

Mack nearly dropped his small cup. "Missing? Is he sure?"

"We don't know," I said. "Reese went with him to interview the lady who insists he's disappeared."

Kate eyed Mack over the rim of her mug as she took a sip. "Why? Do you know Kris?"

"Kris Kringle Jingle?" Mack looked at her as if her question was absurd. "Of course we know him." He leaned his head back and bellowed for Buster, then turned back to us. "When it isn't the holidays, he's one of our local laborers. Mostly loading the vans and unloading shipments."

Buster appeared from the door leading into the back of the shop, his face lighting up when he saw us. "Sorry about that. I was on the phone trying to get more holly for Greta Van Strubbel's party." He pushed the black biker goggles further up on his bald head. "Although I'm not sure how the holly and berry theme is going to play if it hits eighty degrees."

I didn't know how both men were still completely decked out in black leather pants and thick jackets emblazoned with Road Riders for

Jesus patches when it was so warm. Just looking at them made me sweat, but I didn't say anything.

"Tell us about it," Kate said. "Saturday's wedding has an icicle theme, remember?"

"Did you know about Kris?" Mack said to Buster.

"Kris Kringle Jingle?" Buster asked, stroking one hand down his brown goatee. "No, what?"

Mack waved a beefy hand toward me and Kate. "The ladies say he's missing."

"To be perfectly accurate," Kate said, "Fern is the one who says he's missing. And he's getting his information from a woman named Jeannie."

Mack drained his espresso in a single gulp. "That would explain why we didn't see him yesterday. He usually passes by and belts out a verse of 'The Little Drummer Boy.'"

Buster blinked hard a few times. More evidence that Buster and Mack were softies, despite their intimidating appearance. "That song gets us every time." He swiped at his eyes. "Do they think something has happened to him?"

"Reese went with Fern to talk to this Jeannie woman."

Mack put a hand to his heart. "That's a relief. I know your fiancé will be able to find him."

"If he's missing," I said. "It's so warm, he might just be taking a break at home instead of having to be out in a heavy Santa suit in this heat."

"Home?" Buster cocked his head at me. "Kris doesn't have a home."

Kate's mug clattered on the table. "What do you mean he doesn't have a home?"

"An apartment then?" I asked, lowering my own mug before I took a drink.

Mack shook his head. "He moves around the shelters, and he sometimes rents a cheap motel room, especially when it gets really cold or he works a lot of jobs for us, but Kris has been homeless for years."

I remembered that Buster and Mack often employed the neighborhood homeless when they needed extra labor, paying them under the table with cash and feeding them well throughout the day.

Buster shoved his hands into the pockets of his snug leather pants. "He can usually be found at one of the shelters. Have they searched all those yet?"

"I don't know." I glanced at Kate, who looked just as shocked as I was. I'd seen Kris Kringle Jingle charming people with holiday songs for years, and never once had I suspected he was homeless. Now that I knew the singing Santa lived on the street, I found my own stomach tightening with worry. Suddenly, our weddings didn't seem like the most important thing in the world.

CHAPTER 5

I pushed against my front door, but it only slid forward a few inches. Glancing back at Kate, who held her high heels in one hand after the climb up three flights of stairs, I sighed. "This is not a good sign."

"Hold on a second," Richard called out from the crack in the door. "I need to move this so you can get inside."

After a notable amount of heaving and groaning, the door opened. If I weren't absolutely sure I'd walked into the correct stone-fronted apartment building and up the right number of stairs, I would have thought I was in the wrong place.

"Holy holly berries," Kate whispered as she stared through the doorframe, obviously still under the influence of Buster and Mack.

Even though Kate and I had only been gone a couple of hours, my apartment didn't look remotely like I'd left it. The single plastic crate Richard had arrived with had been joined by a stack of glass racks, more plastic crates, and piles of empty cardboard boxes all pushed into the hallway. Richard had clearly gotten a few deliveries after we'd left, and I was both impressed and shocked he'd actually had rental furniture hauled up to my fourth-floor apartment. At least, I hoped it was rental.

The yellow twill sofa and overstuffed chair that comprised the bulk of my living room furniture were gone, as was the beige rug that covered the hardwood floors. In their place were a stylish gray sofa and a pair of pickle wood French chairs upholstered in a gray-and-white chevron pattern. My glass coffee table remained, but the paperwork was gone. It was now topped with a pair of rattan trays arranged with stacks of slipcovered books, bowls of moss balls, and milk glass vases filled with white orchids.

My dining room table had been cleared, draped in a linen I recognized as "White Etched Velvet" from Party Settings rental company and fully set as if I were having a dinner party for eight. Matte silver chargers were topped with white plates, and a gray hemstitched linen napkin was banded around the top plate. Cut glassware and ornate silverware completed the look.

The Christmas tree, which had been sparsely decorated, now stood covered from tip to trunk in ivory, silver, and gold. An ivory crushed velvet ribbon wrapped around the tree as a garland and glass ball ornaments reflected the twinkle of the white lights. Even the base was swathed in a silver crushed velvet skirt and surrounded by boxes wrapped in gold paper.

"I thought you were adding a few design elements," I said, hearing my voice crack. "Where's all my stuff?"

"Not to worry, darling." Richard bustled forward and took me by the elbow. "Your furniture is still here. It's in the back."

"The back?" Kate stepped inside tentatively, as if she wasn't sure about the new version of my apartment. "Where in the back? On the fire escape?"

Richard gave her a side-eye glance. "Of course not. As much as that tired, old stuff might deserve it, I did not relegate it to the fire escape. The couch is in the bedroom and the chair is in the office."

I cast a glance down my hallway. Neither the bedroom nor the office had tons of extra space, so I was afraid to see where exactly the furniture had gone.

"And all this is for...?" I prompted.

"The photo shoot, of course." Richard threw his arms wide. "If the magazine is going to photograph you in your Georgetown apartment, we can't have pictures of you and Kate sitting on a saggy old couch covered in pizza stains."

I understood his logic, but the new furniture looked too chic to sit on. And what kind of person kept a dining table fully set? I knew I would have a hard time looking like I was at home in a place that was decidedly not me.

He patted my arm. "Trust me. All the magazine shoots are like this. No one actually lives in houses that look like the ones in *Architectural Digest*. Everything is staged to some degree."

"This is definitely some degree," Kate mumbled.

"So I'm supposed to live with this until the photo shoot?" I asked, wondering what Reese would think when he saw the new and improved look. This was definitely not a living room where you kicked your feet up onto the coffee table anymore. I twisted around as I scanned the room. "Where's the TV?"

Richard jerked a thumb behind him. "In your bedroom. It made the room look too butch."

"Problem solved," Kate said, poking at one of the glassless silver geometric terrariums on the coffee table. "This is definitely where testosterone goes to die."

"You won't have to suffer very long," Richard said, flouncing off toward the kitchen. "The shoot is tomorrow morning, and I can have everything removed by the afternoon."

"Tomorrow morning?" I repeated. "You didn't tell me the shoot was so soon."

"No need to drag things out, am I right?" Richard said. "Anyway, tomorrow was the only time slot the photographer had. If we'd waited, you'd miss getting into the next issue."

I did a quick mental rundown of the week's schedule. We didn't have any meetings scheduled the next morning, but I worried that the confirmation calls for Saturday's wedding were getting pushed off again. I usually blocked out a full day leading up to a wedding just so Kate and I could focus on the last-minute details and go over the paperwork for a final time.

Kate shrugged. "I guess it's better we get it out of the way. Do we know what we're wearing?"

I almost smacked my forehead as I thought about the jam-packed dry-cleaning bag hanging in my closet. Did I have anything clean to wear? Come to think of it, did I own anything stylish enough for a magazine feature? "Should we go with all black, since that's what we usually wear on a wedding day?"

Richard groaned loudly. "Black again? I'm sure you two can come up with something a little less predictable than black."

"But it's DC," I said, knowing that a black dress might be my only unwrinkled option. "Everyone in DC wears black, even to weddings."

Richard's head appeared in the open space between the kitchen and living room. "Which is why you need to wear something else. *Anything* else."

Kate leaned close to me. "Don't worry. I'll take care of wardrobe."

I eyed her. "Do I need to remind you that microminis and J. Lo necklines do not scream 'elite wedding planner'?"

Before my assistant could make a face at me, I heard a sharp intake of breath behind us.

"I would ask if you've been robbed," Fern said as he walked in, "but it's rare that burglars leave the place looking better than before."

Reese followed him, his eyes wide. "Um, babe?"

"I know, I know," I said, before he could ask. "It's all Richard's doing for the magazine shoot, but it will be gone by tomorrow."

"You're doing a magazine shoot tomorrow?" Fern asked, fluttering his fingers at his throat. "And you didn't ask me to do your hair?"

"Richard just told us about it," Kate said. "Are you free tomorrow morning?"

"For a magazine shoot?" Fern grinned. "Of course I am. If I have any society hussies booked at the salon, I'll just reschedule them. They can get bleached blonde another day."

"You know, the people who said things would get routine after we moved in together could not have been more wrong," Reese said, letting out a breath.

"Not everyone has my friends," I reminded him, taking his hand in mine. "How did it go with Jeannie?"

His expression went from bemused to serious. "I took a statement from her. She seems pretty credible, and I feel confident she told us the truth."

"So Kris Kringle Jingle is missing?"

"It seems so, and Jeannie is convinced that something bad has happened to him," my fiancé said. "She says he was acting nervous the day before he vanished, and he told her that he'd seen something he shouldn't have."

"But he didn't say exactly what?" I asked.

Reese shook his head. "It's not much to go on, but I issued a BOLO for Kris. Luckily, people take a lot of photos with him during the holidays, so I have a good description and a decent image."

"Be on the lookout," Fern mouthed to Kate, with a nudge.

"I know what BOLO means," she said. "We do have cops show up to about half our weddings, remember?"

I tried to ignore her statement, and the fact that it was sort of true.

"Did you know he was homeless?" I asked Reese. "Buster and Mack use him as seasonal labor and they told us he usually rotates through the shelters, but occasionally gets a motel room."

"I knew. Did you know he refuses to take money for singing Christmas carols? Jeannie says it was his way of thanking people for helping him out during the year."

Now that I thought about it, I'd never noticed him asking for money. It was probably one of the reasons I hadn't guessed he was homeless. Concern for the singing Santa gnawed at the back of my mind again, but I told myself that Reese was on the case.

"Is that the office phone?" Kate asked as a muffled ringing came from down the hall.

"Yep," I said, hurrying toward it and pushing open the door to Wedding Belles headquarters. My mouth fell open when I realized that the overstuffed chair that used to sit across from my couch now took up almost every square inch of floor space in my home office.

The room had not been spacious to start with--the desk, office chair, high bookshelf, and tall filing cabinet leaving enough room on the floor for us to store client supplies and assemble gift bags. Richard had shoved the chair far enough into the room so the door could close, and had stacked everything from the floor into the chair. The only way

I could get to the ringing phone on the desk was to dive for it or somehow clamber over the chair that faced away from me.

"Remind me to kill you later," I yelled to Richard as I gingerly stepped onto the back of the chair and attempted to keep my balance. Edging from the back to the arm, I managed to crab walk my way from the upholstered chair to my swivel office chair, collapsing into it and picking up the phone.

"Wedding Belles," I said, steadying my breath. "This is Annabelle."

"You're dead," the voice on the other end said.

My stomach churned as I realized that I knew the voice. Very well.

CHAPTER 6

"You're sure it was Brianna on the phone?" Kate asked, sitting on a stool next to mine the next morning and sipping from a to-go cup of coffee.

We'd positioned the high stools in front of my living room window to get the most natural morning light, and because the sliver of space was the only place in my apartment that wasn't overly staged and styled. My living room had been transformed from frumpy and functional to ornate and over-the-top, and I hardly recognized it.

"Of course I'm sure." I held a bottle of cold Mocha Frappuccino in my lap as Fern sprayed a puff of hairspray on the back of my hair. "First of all, it sounded exactly like her, Southern accent and all. Secondly, who else hates us enough to threaten murder, and probably most damning, I heard someone in the background say her name."

"Amateur," Fern muttered.

"Who's Brianna?" Carl asked as he peered at Kate's face through black-framed, hipster glasses, then began dabbing foundation on her cheeks.

"I forget you've been out of the wedding scene," I said, sliding my gaze over to the makeup artist with short, dark hair and colorful tattoos swirling down both arms.

Although Carl had been one of my original go-to makeup artists, he'd stopped taking weddings for several years in order to serve as the first lady's personal makeup artist. Because the job had involved traveling around the world with her, locking in weddings months out had been impossible. But since the change in the administration, he was now available for weddings again, and we'd even been able to pull in this last-minute favor.

It was a Wedding Belles rule to only hire nice people--sometimes easier said than done in a business with plenty of divas--and Carl fit that bill to a tee. Not only was he a talented makeup artist, he was as sweet and humble as they came, despite his famous client catapulting him into the limelight.

"You're lucky you don't know her," Kate said, her eyes closed as Carl patted something over her lids. "She's all Instagram smoke and mirrors."

He straightened up and assessed Kate's face. "And she threatened to kill you? Why?"

"We have a bit of a complicated relationship with her," I said, shifting on the stool as Fern pulled a round brush through my hair.

Fern let out another blast of hairspray. "That floozy is just jealous of our girls. She's been trying to spread rumors about them ever since she arrived."

I fought the urge to twist around and gape at Fern. Bold words from the man who'd spread the story of Brianna using her wedding planning business as a front for a high-end call girl service. Although I appreciated his loyalty, Fern had only fanned the flames of our feud.

"It's complicated," I said, "but she does seem to have it in for us."

"But why call out of the blue and threaten your life?" Kate asked.

"She called the Wedding Belles line," I reminded her, taking a swig of my cold coffee as Fern stopped brushing. "The threat might not have been just for me."

"Thanks for that," Kate said. "But why now? Most people get *less* vindictive over the holidays."

"Speak for yourself," Richard said, emerging from my kitchen behind us. "Anyone who's waited in line for a photo with Santa deserves to be homicidal."

"I doubt Brianna was having a bad reaction from waiting in line to see Santa." Especially since she was a single twentysomething. "Wait a second. How do you know anything about waiting in line to get a photo with Santa?"

"You don't think I'm going to let the fisherman's sweater I got Hermès in Ireland go to waste, do you? He's very photogenic, you know."

"Who's Hermès?" Carl whispered as Richard bustled around the dining table, no doubt putting the final touches on the completely unrealistic tablescape.

"His dog," Kate whispered back.

"If we eliminate holiday stress from the equation, there must be a reason for her to be mad enough to call and threaten us," I said, trying to get back on topic.

"And she didn't say *why* we were dead?" Kate asked, coughing as Carl dusted her face liberally with powder.

I shook my head. "Just that we were dead and she'd get us back."

"And nothing unusual has happened in the past few days?" Carl asked, bending over his pop-up table arranged neatly with palettes and pencils.

I nibbled the corner of my mouth. "I wouldn't say that. We did book a last-minute New Year's Eve wedding."

"And learned that Kris Kringle Jingle might be missing," Kate added.

Richard clattered a plate behind me. "The New Year's Eve wedding. Didn't you say the couple fired their first planner?"

Kate snapped her fingers. "He's right. They did, but they didn't tell us who the first planner was."

A feeling of dread came over me. "I'll bet it was Brianna. She probably heard we were taking it over and thinks we stole the wedding from her."

"It's not your fault that she has no clue what she's doing," Richard said. "Just because you can take a decent photo of yourself in cute shoes holding a cup of coffee, does not mean you can plan a wedding. What is wrong with these Millennials?"

"Hey," Kate said. "Not all Millennials are as awful as Brianna."

"If it is Brianna, what do we do about it?" I asked, gulping down the last of my chocolately, cold coffee and feeling grateful for both the caffeine and the sugar.

"Do about it?" Richard huffed out a breath as he came to stand in front of me, both hands on his hips. "You don't do anything. It's not like you're going to turn down the wedding, and you can't let petty people change the way you live your life. The more successful you become, the more jealous people you'll have to deal with. Trust me, darling. It's a cross I've had to bear for years."

I grinned at him, comforted by both his faith in me and my continuing success and his pep talk. "You're right. I can't let one person affect me so much."

"That being said," Richard waved one hand in the direction of my front door, "I might consider adding an extra dead bolt or two and perhaps one of those doorbell cameras."

"You should add that just for Leatrice," Kate muttered.

"I'm sure your hunky fiancé has it under control," Fern said. "I know I wouldn't worry if I lived with a cop that looked like that. You just know he's packing."

My cheeks warmed as Richard rolled his eyes and flounced back into the kitchen.

"I'm sure you're worrying over nothing," Carl said, his voice low and calm as he swirled pink blush over Kate's cheeks. "Most people are more bark than bite anyway. You just keep doing the good work you always do and don't worry about the rest. Karma will take care of that."

I smiled at Carl. I'd missed his even-keeled manner over the past few years, although it was easy to understand why the first lady had loved having him around. "You're right. Thanks."

"Anytime." He squeezed my shoulder. "Now, did you say something about Kris Kringle Jingle being missing?"

"Do you know him?" I asked.

He nodded as he stepped back, sizing up Kate's face and adding more blush to one cheek. "I worked at a Georgetown salon for years, remember? Kris Kringle Jingle always popped into the salon in December to say hello and sing a quick song."

Fern chuckled. "He does that in my salon, too. You should see my old society ladies light up."

I closed my eyes as Fern unleashed a cloud of spray over my head. "Did you know he's homeless?"

"No." Carl sounded surprised. "I don't think he ever asked us for money."

Fern stopped spraying. "He doesn't do Kris Kringle Jingle for money. It's his way of thanking the Georgetown residents."

"Speaking of Georgetown residents," Kate said as Buster and Mack bustled in behind us, the jangling chains on their leather clothing alerting us to their arrival.

"Sorry we're late," Mack called out. "It's been a crazy morning."

"Don't worry," I said. In truth, I hadn't known they were coming over at all.

"Thank heavens," Richard said. "I was worried I'd have to fashion some sort of candle centerpiece if you didn't get the flowers here in time."

I twisted around to see that Mack and Buster held a massive floral centerpiece between them. I shot Richard a look. "You made them bring flowers?"

Richard pressed a hand to his heart. "You expected me to set a table without fresh flowers? Really, Annabelle."

I'm sorry, I mouthed to my burly friends before Fern turned my head back so I faced forward.

"We're happy to do it," Mack said. "We were just running short on labor this morning, so it took twice as long to load the delivery trucks."

Even though I couldn't see, I could hear the two men setting the arrangement on the dining table and Richard fussing over it and moving glassware.

"Our usual guys were involved in the search," Buster added.

Mack let out a long sigh. "Once we drop this off, we're going to head back and join them."

"The search?" I wanted to turn back around but Fern held my head in place.

"For Kris," Buster said. "The homeless in Georgetown have organized their own search party to look for him."

I thought about the BOLO my fiancé had issued for Kris. I hoped between law enforcement and the search party, they'd locate him soon. It wouldn't feel like the holidays in Georgetown without the singing Santa.

"Well, this isn't good," Kate said.

"Agreed," I said. "I'd hoped Kris would have turned up by now."

"Not that, *this*," Kate stared down at the phone in her lap as Carl leaned over his makeup table, swirling an eye shadow brush in a small pot of pale pink powder. "You know how our New Year's Eve bride already had her venue set? Well, I just got a text from the space manager, Trista. She comes to the wedding planner assistant happy hours. Apparently, Brianna signed the contract for the client, so it's technically *her* rental, and she just told them that the New Year's Eve event is no longer a wedding, it's a party for Brides by Brianna."

My stomach dropped. "Can she do that?" I asked, even though I knew that she could. If she signed the contract, she was the client. I'd thought our new bride and groom had signed all their own contracts, but it looked like Brianna ran her business differently than we did. I assumed she did it so she could mark everything up, a practice I'd never believed in, but I knew some of our colleagues made a pretty penny doing it.

"According to Trista, it's already done," Kate said with a groan.

Fern made a disapproving noise in the back of his throat. "Looks like it's time to revive the tales about Madame Brianna."

I was too worried to even attempt to talk Fern out of it. With only three weeks to go, our new wedding was back to square one. How were we going to find an available venue for New Year's Eve on top of everything else?

CHAPTER 7

"Try not to look like you're being held at gunpoint," Richard said, standing a few feet away as Kate and I posed on the sofa.

I sat on one end, wearing the surprisingly appropriate pale green wrap dress Kate had chosen for me, while she perched on the armrest in a not-too-short winter white sheath. We both wore significantly more makeup than we usually did--including false lashes--but I knew it wouldn't look as dramatic in photos.

"Which one of us are you talking to?" I asked, trying not to let my smile falter.

"You," Kate, Richard, and Fern all said at once.

I let out a breath and allowed my shoulders to sag. "Sorry. I can't stop thinking about the New Year's Eve wedding."

"It's okay." The female photographer lowered her camera. "Take a minute while I readjust the lights."

Fern rushed over holding a hair pick and a can of hairspray. "At least your style is holding up, sweetie."

I gave him a quick once-over. Instead of the black pants and shirt he'd been wearing that morning, he now had on beige pants tucked into high black boots, a matching belted jacket, and a black beret. "Did you change?"

Richard emitted an exasperated sigh as he joined us. "This is not a movie set, and you're not an old Hollywood director." He turned to face me, as Fern huffed something about Richard not having vision, then began fluffing Kate's hair. "I told you, darling. Don't worry. I'm making calls around town. If there's an available venue for New Year's Eve, I'll find it."

"But what if there isn't? It's bad enough that we're going to have to reprint invitations and have them rushed, but now we might not have a location to put on the invitations."

When I'd talked to the bride earlier, she'd been livid that her former planner had taken her venue. I'd been able to calm her down, but knowing brides the way I did, that calm wouldn't last long if we couldn't find a new site. Fast.

Richard took my hand and gave it an awkward pat. "You worrying and making the photo shoot take even longer than it should isn't going to help anyone. I know it's hard, but you need to channel some of that patented Annabelle Archer Zen. Focus on nothing but getting these photos right. Then you can worry about the wedding venue."

"And the wedding on Saturday and my engagement party?"

"Both of which are already planned," Kate reminded me.

"That's why you have a team, right?" Richard asked. "No one can do everything single-handedly, even though you like to think you can."

I managed a smile. Richard knew me too well. I did have a tendency to try to take on everything myself, even though time and time again I needed my friends to pull it all off. "You're right. Sorry I freaked out. I'm just rattled that a colleague would go after us and a client so blatantly."

"Brianna is a not a colleague." Richard's voice was low. "If you ask me, she's a wannabe who's gotten too big for her britches."

"Whatever she is," Kate said as Fern sprayed a final cloud of hairspray over her bob and moved away, "she's a horn in our side."

I suppressed an urge to laugh at the mental image of horns sprouting from our sides. "Or a thorn."

"Intolerable." Richard waved his hands in front of his face to disperse the high-end spray, although he could have just as easily been referring to Kate's habit of mangling expressions, which I sometimes suspected she continued to do just for his benefit.

Kate shrugged. "The only reason she can take over the venue and have a personal party there is because she doesn't have a New Year's Eve wedding. I'm sure no one important will go to her party."

"Not when we hire them for your client's wedding," Richard said with a wicked grin. "And Miss Malaprop is right. Brianna doesn't have any business. I mean, she's never once called me, and I'm the best caterer in the city."

I knew that Brianna would never call Richard because she knew we were best friends, but I didn't want to remind him that I was a reason he was missing out on business, even if he was correct and there wasn't much to be had.

"Ready?" the photographer asked from a few feet away.

I straightened my shoulders. "Let's do this."

Richard moved quickly out of the shot, standing next to Fern and Carl behind the light stand. He returned to tapping away on his phone, and I knew he was sending out his feelers for a venue. Richard had been in the DC wedding industry for far longer than I had and knew all the movers and shakers, as well as those who were off the radar. If anyone could track down a venue in a matter of hours, it would be him.

"We need to do something about Brianna," Kate said between shots, her face frozen in a smile. "She's gone from annoying to problematic to disastrous for our business."

"Chins down, ladies," the photographer said, moving in closer.

I lowered my chin as the shutter clicked rapidly. "Like what? We had no idea she was the planner our new client fired or that she'd signed their contracts. I feel like this is an isolated occurrence."

"What about all the times she spread rumors about us being murder magnets?"

"To be fair," I said, "that's kind of true."

The photographer moved to the right as she continued snapping. "Now turn your heads toward me."

"We haven't been involved in a murder in months," Kate said, sounding affronted. "Practically a lifetime."

I almost giggled. What did it say about us that we considered eight months without finding a dead body to be a good run?

"Perfect," the photographer called out. "Those are great smiles!"

"I agree that Brianna has been nothing but trouble for us, but it's not like we can run her out of town on a rail," I said.

"I don't care what she's on, as long as she leaves," Kate said. "Fern will have some ideas, I'm sure."

I glanced at Fern, fully expecting him to be holding a megaphone by his side and yelling 'Action'. "We don't have time to add 'blood feud' to this week's to-do list."

"Fine," she sighed. "But don't expect Brianna to back down. That Southern belle is a Southern bi--"

"That's it, ladies." The photographer lowered her camera. "I've got what I need."

"Thank you," I said, sinking back on the couch.

Kate flopped down next to me, her eyes sweeping the room. "This new look is kind of growing on me, although this couch is definitely not as comfortable as your old one."

"That's called structural integrity," Richard said, walking over. "Which those sad, old, yellow couch cushions barely have."

"Say what you will about my furniture," I said. "It's comfortable. I don't think I could live in a place as perfect as this."

"Pearls unto swine," Richard muttered, turning on his heel and walking over to thank the photographer.

"I hope you have plans to do something fun later," Carl said, joining us on the couch. "You're all made up for date night."

Kate raised her hand. "I do. I'd never let these long lashes go to waste."

"Every night is date night for some people," I said.

Kate twisted to face me. "If you tell me you and Reese are staying in and ordering Thai again, I'm going to go ballistic."

"I don't know what we're doing. I didn't think I'd be so done up, so we didn't even discuss it."

Carl nudged me. "Make him take you somewhere fabulous. You've got the smoky eyes to pull it off."

Kate held up a warning finger. "And not a sports bar. I've seen how much your fiancé loves ESPN."

It would be a shame to sit at home after having the former first lady's makeup artist do my face, although I didn't know how Reese would react to seeing me with such dramatic eyes. He was used to seeing me with barely a swipe of mascara and just a touch of face powder.

"Speak of the very attractive devil," Kate said as the door opened, and Reese stepped inside.

His eyebrows lifted as he took in the lights stands positioned throughout the room, Richard standing off to the side on his phone, Fern chatting with the photographer as she packed up her camera, and the multiple makeup cases and stools gathered by the door.

I gave him a wave, and his eyes widened.

"Is that your fiancé?" Carl asked in a hushed voice.

"Mmm hmm," Kate answered for me. "And he's a cop. A detective, actually. He doesn't always look so scary, though."

I stood as I registered the intense look on his face. We hadn't been living together for too long, but I knew when he was concerned.

"How did the shoot go?" he asked, forcing a smile as I took his hand. "You look really pretty."

"Thanks," I said. "It was good. What's wrong?"

He released a breath. "That obvious, huh?" He scraped a hand through his hair. "It's about Kris."

"Buster and Mack said they were joining all Kris's homeless friends to search for him. Maybe having all those people looking will help the search."

Reese tightened his grip on my hand. "Actually, we found something."

My stomach lurched. "Kris?"

"Not exactly," he said. "We found his Santa suit covered in blood."

CHAPTER 8

"I should tell Jeannie," Fern said, holding a cold compress to his head as he reclined on the couch.

We'd all been upset to learn that Kris Kringle Jingle's Santa suit had been found covered in blood, but Fern had taken it especially hard, slumping to the floor and having to be carried to the couch, where he lay sprawled from one end to the other. Kate had rescued his fallen beret from the floor and was now fanning him with it.

Amid the hysteria, both the magazine photographer and Carl had made their excuses and left, so it was just the five of us.

"I suspect she's heard by now," Reese said, sitting on the edge of one of the upholstered armchairs, his elbows leaning on his knees. "Word spreads pretty quickly on the streets."

Fern emitted a choked sob and mumbled something as Kate patted his shoulder and fanned faster.

"Tell us again where you found it," Richard called from the kitchen where I knew he was quietly packing up his supplies. Not even a bloody Santa suit could slow Richard's instinct to tidy, although I knew he was trying to be discreet.

Reese glanced down at his pocket-sized notebook. "Shoved in a dumpster in one of the alleys off M Street. It appeared sometime between late last night and this morning, because the beat cop didn't report seeing it on his patrol last night, and it was hanging out of the top."

I paced a small circle behind the couch. "Just because the suit was found doesn't mean Kris is dead."

Reese nodded solemnly. "No, but there was a lot of blood. If whoever was wearing the suit isn't dead, they're severely wounded."

Fern made another strangled sound.

"Why would someone hurt him, then dump the suit separately from the body?" I asked.

My fiancé shrugged. "Maybe they're hoping his body won't be identified when it's found."

"So you guys are searching for a body or a person?" Kate's voice was low and her brow furrowed.

Reese didn't answer.

My throat constricted, and I blew out a breath. Who would want to hurt or kill a man who dressed as Santa and sang songs to cheer people up? It wasn't like he was panhandling, so he wouldn't have any cash on him for muggers. And according to Reese, he didn't have any sort of criminal record, so it wasn't like his past was catching up to him. As far as I could tell, Kris was innocent. If this had to do with something he thought he saw, whatever it was must have been pretty bad.

"This is awful. The holidays won't feel the same without Kris Kringle Jingle," Kate said, giving voice to what we all probably felt. "They should just cancel Christmas in Georgetown this year."

I knew what she meant. Knowing that Santa was missing and might be dead didn't put you in the holiday spirit.

Richard inhaled sharply from the kitchen. "Cancel Christmas? Are you out of your mind? I've got a half dozen holiday parties to cater in the next week. People overeating during the holidays is the only thing that gets my business through the horrific month of January when everyone is on a diet."

Fern bolted upright and the cold washcloth flopped onto his lap. "I hate to admit it, but Richard is right. Canceling Christmas is the last thing Kris would have wanted. He was all about getting people into the spirit of the season. Besides, we don't know he'd dead."

"Who would have had it in for him?" I asked, walking around to face Fern.

Fern stood, and the damp cloth fell from his lap to the floor. "I'm not the person who knew him best."

Reese flipped a page in his notebook. "Jeannie insisted he didn't have any enemies. She said he got along with everyone--business owners and homeless alike."

"So it has to be connected to whatever it was he thought he saw," I said.

"I need to see her." Fern unbelted his beige jacket and tossed it onto the couch. "She'll be upset."

Reese stood. "I'll come with you."

"You're not going without me." I looked around the apartment for my purse. Where had Richard hidden it when he'd purged the space of anything practical?

"Dressed like that?" Kate waved a hand at my celadon-green dress made of silk shantung, then her gaze dropped to my heels. "You'll break your neck in two seconds."

I wanted to argue that I could walk in heels, but I knew she was right. I never wore heels for any significant stretch of time anymore, and the three-inch pumps would have me limping after only a block on the uneven Georgetown sidewalks. Plus, I was dressed for a society garden party, not to go traipsing around the city. I headed down the hall. "It will only take me a minute to change."

Richard poked his head out of the kitchen doorway as I passed. "I suppose you're leaving me here to clean up?"

"You *are* the only one who knows which rentals came from which company," I said.

He let out a sigh. "Fine, but frankly, this new look is growing on me. You're sure you don't want to leave the furniture as is?"

I opened my bedroom door and crawled over the couch that now took up every bit of floor space, my feet sinking into the sagging cushions. Even though my original furniture was worn and many years from stylish, it was comfortable. The furniture Richard had brought in for the shoot may have looked chic, but it was not the kind of stuff you cuddled up on.

"I'm sure," I called out, clambering over the back of the couch and opening my closet door as I untied my wrap dress. As promised, I quickly changed into a pair of jeans and a T-shirt and climbed back over the couch, holding the photo shoot dress I'd tucked back into the garment bag it had arrived in.

"I believe this is yours." I met Kate in the hallway outside the kitchen entrance and handed her the bag.

"Technically, it belongs to Rent the Runway, but who's quibbling? It's mine for another twenty-four hours."

Although I understood the concept of renting designer fashion--after all, men had been doing it with tuxedos for years--it still gave me pause that so many stylish young women in DC didn't own a thing they wore. According to Kate, some of her friends had virtually empty closets but a monthly subscription plan to Rent the Runway. They wore designer clothes that they could never afford, yet owned none of them.

"Do you mind staying here and catching up on the confirmation calls for Saturday?" I asked her.

"Consider it done." She looked down at her white dress. "Besides, I didn't bring good crime investigation clothes."

"We aren't investigating," I said, but stopped when I noticed that both she and Richard wore disbelieving looks on their faces. I cast a quick glance at my fiancé, who stood near the front door. "I'm with Reese. Even if I wanted to, how much poking around could I do?"

Richard stood in the doorway to the kitchen, his hands on his hips and one toe tapping on the linoleum. "If there's a way, you'll find it."

I held up three fingers. "I'm not doing anything but supporting Fern as he talks to Jeannie. No investigating. Scout's honor."

"You know," Kate said, tilting her head at me then glancing at Richard. "I think she actually believes what she's saying."

"Which goes to support my belief that anyone who works with brides day in and day out can't help but be delusional," Richard said.

"I'm not delusional," I said. "And I'm not getting sucked into another investigation, especially not this week. We don't have time for it."

"That's what you say every time, Annabelle." Richard shook his head. "And before you know it, we're all poking around for clues, breaking into suspects' hotel rooms, and running from deranged killers."

Kate held up a finger. "One hotel room, and we had the key, so technically it wasn't breaking and entering."

I motioned with my hands for both of them to keep it down. "Not so loud. Reese doesn't know all the details about our trip to Ireland, and I'd like to keep it that way."

"I'm sure you would," Richard said. "Just remember. It's two weeks before Christmas, and you've got a big wedding on Saturday with a lavish rehearsal dinner the night before, as well as a wedding to plan from start to finish by New Year's Eve." He took a gulp of air. "Not to mention the fact that you still don't have a venue for it. This is no time to play Nancy Drew."

My pulse raced at the thought of how much work we had to do. He was right. I had no time to spare. "Don't worry. I'm with my fiancé. You know how he feels about me poking around in his cases."

"I don't know, Annie," Kate said, tapping one finger on her chin. "He seems to have gotten so used to you meddling that he doesn't even notice it anymore. He even planned one of our criminal-catching schemes."

Richard nodded solemnly. "It's Stockholm Syndrome."

I shot him a look. "Stockholm Syndrome? You mean when a captive becomes sympathetic or emotionally attached to their captor. Who's the captor in this scenario? Me?"

Richard shrugged, his face the picture of innocence. "I'm only saying that you may have used your feminine wiles to make your fiancé more tolerant of your crime-solving fetish."

"My feminine wiles?"

"Yeah, I'm not sure about that," Kate said, tilting her head at me. "Generally speaking, Annabelle doesn't have feminine wiles."

"Thank you." I hesitated. "I think."

I glanced over at Fern standing with Reese, his face ashen. "Listen. I'll be back before you know it, ready to focus on work."

I joined Reese and Fern, giving a backward wave to my friends as we left the apartment. I would show them that I could stay out of a case, I thought. Then again, this was Santa we were talking about.

CHAPTER 9

We stopped at the corner of M Street, and I jumped back so a lady with a double stroller wouldn't run over my toes. It was afternoon in Georgetown and the weather was sunny and warm, which meant everyone was out. The streets bustled with shoppers and tourists, people weaving around each other down the brick sidewalks holding colorful paper shopping bags with ribbon handles. Wreaths topped each of the tall lampposts, and shop windows featured holiday displays, although the icy blues (and even the bright greens and reds) seemed incongruous with the almost summertime weather.

Despite the temperature, the neighborhood looked decked out for the season, and holiday music drifted out from various shops. The tinny notes of "Santa Baby" mingled with the sound of a Salvation Army bell ringer at the end of the next block. I inhaled deeply and could smell the rich aroma of coffee, reminding me that in DC, I was never more than a few feet away from a Starbucks at any given time. Or at least it felt that way. My stomach growled. I wouldn't mind a peppermint mocha, even though I knew we were not here to get coffee.

"So where does Jeannie usually hang out?" I asked.

"Depends." Fern scanned the crowds. "At the holidays, she likes to stay out of the way since it's such a madhouse, but Clyde's is a favorite. They give her coffee and lunch most days."

"That's where she was yesterday," Reese said, pulling me close as a group of giggling teenaged girls barreled by us without looking up.

"Then Clyde's it is." I started heading toward the popular restaurant, using the massive nutcrackers they put outside their restaurant each December as a visual guide.

We passed Starbucks, and I sucked in the addictive scent, promising myself that I'd treat myself on the way back. I would need the caffeine for the rest of the day, anyway.

"Annabelle!"

Mack's deep voice made me turn as he came out of the chain coffee shop behind us, carrying a cardboard holder filled with to-go cups and a handful of paper bags I assumed were filled with pastries.

"Hey," I said, noticing his eyes were rimmed red. "I didn't expect to see you here. Don't you usually go to Baked and Wired on your block, that is if you aren't brewing your own?"

He took a shaky breath. "I'm getting coffees and snacks for some of Kris's friends who were helping with the search. They're right around the corner, so I didn't want to make them wait." He dropped his voice. "Don't tell Buster I didn't shop local."

I mimed zipping up my lips. "You can count on me."

"Since we've stopped to chat," Fern said, looking longingly in the glass window, "I need a coffee and maybe a scone." He waved a hand in front of his brimming eyes, his voice cracking. "I'm so upset, I'm craving carbs."

Mack watched Fern hurry into the Starbucks. "I know how he feels. I can't believe what they found."

"How did you hear?" Reese asked. "We were going to come find you after we talked to Jeannie."

"One of the fellows who helps us out sometimes, Stanley, was the first person to happen upon the bloody suit."

"Is he okay?" Reese asked.

"A little shaken up," Mack said, shifting from one leg to the other, his leather pants groaning in response. "He and Kris are friends, and they usually worked as a team when they helped us out."

"Has he given a statement already?" Reese asked.

Mack shrugged. "I don't know, but I can ask. Everyone's pretty upset. It would be one thing if they'd found a body, but his Santa suit drenched in blood just makes us all worry about what happened to him and where he is. None of us believe he's dead, but if he was the person in that suit, he must be hurt."

"That's a pretty safe bet," I said. "If he was hurt, do you know anyone he'd turn to or anyplace he might hide?"

Mack rubbed a hand down his goatee. "Aside from Jeannie? I like to think he'd come to us if he needed help, but we haven't seen him."

"And you don't know anyone who would want to hurt Kris?" Reese asked.

Mack shook his head firmly. "He didn't have an enemy in the world. Everyone loved Kris. The police are sure it wasn't another Santa?"

Now it was Reese's turn to shake his head. "His name was written on the inside of the suit in Sharpie."

"You're still looking for him, right?" Mack said, staring intently at my fiancé. "I mean, even though Kris was homeless."

Reese put a hand on Mack's thick, tattooed forearm. "Of course. This case will get just as much attention as any other. I'll make sure of it."

A small smile cracked Mack's face, and he cleared his throat. "Well, I'd better get back to the group."

"Can you let Stanley know I'd like to talk to him?" Reese asked as Mack started to back away.

"We'll probably go back to Lush if you want to stop by later," Mack called out over the din of the crowd before he disappeared around the corner.

"Did you know Buster and Mack employed so many homeless people?" Reese asked.

I thought about it. "I've definitely seen them use homeless crew to unload their vans at churches, especially at New York Avenue Presbyterian and St. Matthew's Cathedral. I didn't know they used them so often at the shop, but I usually don't see the back end of their operation. Knowing Buster and Mack, I'm not surprised."

"Me either," Reese said. "Those two certainly aren't what you'd expect when you first look at them, are they?"

"Is anyone?"

"That's it," Fern said, pushing open the glass door and emerging from the coffee shop. Crumbs fell from his mouth as he thrust a cardboard drink holder and small paper bag at me. "This day is officially a disaster."

"What happened?" I asked. "Are they out of skim soy milk?"

"What happened is that I just chugged a full fat latte and ate a blueberry scone." Fern pressed his fingers to his lips. "All this with Kris has pushed me over the edge. I won't be able to fit into my skinny holiday pants if I keep this up."

"You already drank your coffee?" I glanced down at the three paper cups. "So this is...?"

"For you two, of course. And Jeannie." He rolled his eyes at me. "As if I don't know your coffee order, sweetie." He patted Reese's arm. "I pegged you as a plain coffee guy, but I did get you a cake doughnut. You know, since you're a cop."

The corner of Reese's mouth quirked up. "Thanks."

"You're very welcome." Fern spun on his heel. "Now let's go talk to Jeannie before I go back in there and get another scone."

Fern started walking ahead of us toward Clyde's, and I hurried to catch up, pulling the coffee out of the holder and passing it to Reese, along with the doughnut bag. I balanced the holder while dislodging my own hot mocha and dodging the aggressive shoppers. I took a sip as I walked, trying not to spill the warm drink all over me and groaning out loud as I swallowed and realized Fern had asked for extra mocha syrup. He knew me so well.

Fern barely paused at the intersection with Wisconsin Avenue, barreling across only moments before the walk signal started blinking its warning. Reese and I ran to make it before the stream of traffic resumed, my foot touching the other side of the sidewalk as I heard cars rush by behind me.

"If this is what he's like when he drinks regular milk and eats carbs, I'm glad he's usually on a diet," I said to Reese. "I don't know if I could keep up if he was full octane all the time."

I spotted the giant nutcrackers ahead of us, flanking the entrance to the popular restaurant. Towering at least fifteen feet high, the glossy, brightly colored figures jutted out onto the sidewalk in front of the large glass windows of the restaurant. Fern stopped when he reached the wooden and brass doors, waiting for us to catch up. Even before he threw open the door, I could smell the aroma of crab cakes and french fries, probably the place's most popular menu items.

"She should be at the bar," Fern said, holding the door open for us.

I stepped inside and my eyes adjusted to the rich wood of the long bar and the burgundy of the booths stretched down one side of the narrow room. I didn't know what Jeannie looked like, but a quick scan of the bar told me the businessmen and tourists in bright shorts and fanny packs weren't her.

Fern bit the corner of his lip as he took in the restaurant. "Let me talk to the hostess."

He approached a petite woman dressed in black and talked to her in hushed tones.

"Was she at the bar yesterday?" I asked my fiancé, noticing that he hadn't touched the coffee or doughnut.

He nodded, his face set in an unreadable expression.

"She's not here," Fern said when he returned to us. "Hasn't been here all day."

"Is that unusual?" I asked.

"Very." Fern fluttered a hand over his neat ponytail. "The manager slips her cash to sweep the sidewalk every morning. Today's the first day she didn't show."

"Really?" Reese's face turned grim. "In how long?"

"Years," Fern said, his voice quavering as he clutched my arm. "Oh, Annabelle. I have a horrible feeling something's happened to Jeannie, too."

CHAPTER 10

The overhead bell jingled as we walked into Lush, and I breathed in the distinctive scents of pine and cinnamon. Even though the weather outside was far from frightful, Buster and Mack's festively decorated shop smelled every bit like Christmas.

"We're back here," Buster called, and I saw an arm waving above the arrangements of frosted branches and miniature fir trees on the display tables.

As I passed an artfully stacked collection of trendy Homesick candles in colorful boxes, I was reminded that I hadn't even started shopping for gifts for my friends. I wondered how many of them would enjoy a "Jewish Christmas" or "Grandma's Kitchen" scented candle. I picked up a pink box that read "Single, Not Sorry" and described the candle inside as smelling like freedom and fun. I'd have to remember to come back and buy that one for Kate.

Replacing the quirky candle, I led the way to the back of the store where Mack stood at the espresso machine and the long metal table was surrounded by people on the high stools. Some of the faces seemed vaguely familiar, and I suspected I'd seen them unloading the florals at past weddings.

Prue waved at me while bouncing a giggling Merry on her lap and flipping her dirty-blond ponytail out of the baby's reach. "You all look like you need some hot chocolate."

The last thing I needed was another hot drink, but I smiled at Merry's young mother and nodded. "Sure, thanks."

Fern sat on one of the last available barstools, slumping over the table, and Buster looked up at me from where he sat comforting a man in an unseasonably thick flannel shirt. "Is he okay?"

"We struck out with Jeannie," I said.

Fern raised his head. "Because she's gone."

"Gone?" Mack fumbled with the mug he was holding. "What do you mean gone?"

"The staff at Clyde's hasn't seen her today," Reese said. "But that could be because she's been out looking for Kris."

Mack nodded his head, a bit too eagerly. "I'm sure that's it."

Fern gave a sharp shake of his head. "It isn't like Jeannie to be a no-show. Even if she was going to look for Kris, she would have swept the front of Clyde's first."

"Her friend's disappearance could very well have thrown her off her usual routine," Reese said, using his calmest police detective voice. "She was clearly distraught when we talked to her yesterday. That kind of anxiety can cause people to do things they wouldn't normally do or forget things they usually do."

Fern pressed his fingers to his throat. "I hope you're right. She's supposed to come by the salon tomorrow morning before I open for her wash and style, although she only ever wears her hair in a long braid, which is *not* a style."

"I'm sure she'll be there," I said, feigning more confidence than I felt. "She probably heard that Kris's suit was found and is shaken up."

There were mumbles around the table that told me not everyone agreed with me, but Fern sat up straighter. "Maybe you're right. The old girl never misses her hair appointment. It's when she fills me in on all the Georgetown gossip."

"So is that how you know what everyone in Georgetown is up to?" I asked.

Fern smiled. "Of course. Jeannie sees everything that goes on around here."

Mack lumbered over to me and Reese, handing both of us steaming mugs. "We've been talking about what could have happened to Kris. We have quite a few theories about how his suit could have gotten blood on it."

"It could be tomato sauce," a woman with frizzy gray hair said. "Kris loves spaghetti."

I noticed Reese's eyebrow lift. Even the most rookie cop wouldn't mistake spaghetti sauce for blood, but he didn't respond.

"Or he might have gotten a bunch of paint on him and thrown out the suit," someone else called out.

"Does anyone know where he might have gone if he did get hurt?" Reese asked. "Does he have any family in the area?"

"Kris didn't have any family that I know of," Mack said, then turned to the people gathered around the table. "Did he ever mention family to you all?"

Head shakes and low murmurs told us no.

"If he had any family that was still alive, they didn't live here," Prue said. "I think he was originally from somewhere up North. The last time he was in the shop he mentioned that he'd never gotten used to the heat south of the Mason-Dixon."

Reese took his notebook out of his jeans pocket, flipped it open, and began scribbling. "Did he say anything else about his past?"

"Kris didn't focus on the past," a man said from the end of the table. "He always said he was moving forward."

"And paying it forward," a woman with bushy brown hair said, blowing her nose into a tissue. "That's why he put on the costume and sang to people. He liked to give back."

"Not everyone agreed with him on that," a small man with a grizzled beard said almost so quietly I couldn't hear him.

I stepped closer to the man, who seemed to shrink into himself as I approached. "What? What do you mean?"

The man's gaze darted around the group. "I'm saying what we all knew. Not everyone thought Kris should have been taking all the attention and making us look bad."

Heads dropped around the table, and there was a murmur of both agreement and dissent.

"How did he make you look bad?" Reese asked.

The man shrugged, not lifting his head. "He didn't ask for money, so it made it harder for those of us who did. And the Salvation Army bell ringers *really* didn't like him."

I stared at the man even though he wouldn't look up at me. "The other Santas had it in for him?"

Another shrug as he shifted on his stool. "You know they get part of the money they collect. It was hard for them to compete with Kris's singing. I've seen a few of them try to run him off or try to drown him out with their bell."

I exchanged a glance with my fiancé. I'd never given a thought to how Kris Kringle Jingle might impact other Santas or other homeless people, but I supposed it made sense. You could never make everyone happy.

"Thanks," Reese said. "That's helpful. I can also check if he's in the system," Reese said, "but I'm guessing Kris Kringle Jingle wasn't his legal name."

"It's all I ever knew him as," a heavyset, balding man said, his voice high and chirpy.

"I'm assuming you didn't put him on your payroll," Reese said to Mack, "so you never needed any official documents."

Mack shifted from one foot to the other. "That's right. He was strictly freelance and paid in cash."

Reese nodded. "Don't worry. The metropolitan police department has bigger things to worry about than a flower shop helping out the local street population with under-the-table payments."

"That's why you're our favorite cop." Mack let out a breath, but I noticed several of the people at the table stiffen.

"Don't worry," I said. "He's only trying to help figure out what happened to your friend."

"That's right," Reese said. "I want to find Kris."

Fern nudged the bushy-haired woman next to him. "I've worked with him on more than one murder case. He may look like a pretty face, but he'll find our Kris."

Reese ignored Fern's comment, but a flush crept up his neck. "Now, which one of you is Stanley?"

Mack scanned the room, then exchanged a look with Buster. "He was here earlier. Where did he go?"

"Are we talking about the guy who discovered the suit?" I asked, glancing at Reese's pinched face. "Didn't you tell him we needed to talk to him?"

"We did," Buster said, disappearing through the doorway that led to the back office and designer workspace. After a minute, he returned shaking his head. "He's not in the back or in the loading dock or alley."

Mack ran a hand over his bald head. "He looked nervous when we mentioned that a policeman would be stopping by to take his statement. Maybe we shouldn't have mentioned the cop part."

"I don't know why that would be an issue," Buster said. "He already talked to the cops when he gave his statement. Plus, an officer was there when they found the Santa costume. Helped calm him down. An Officer Rogers, I think. I remembered because it reminded me of Mr. Rogers."

"We watch a lot of Mr. Rogers reruns with Merry," Mack said, pressing a hand to his heart. "We love Mr. Rogers."

Reese flipped his notebook closed. "It's all right. Maybe he didn't want to give his statement twice. I can review what he said when I get back to the station."

"That's two people," Fern said.

"Two people?" Prue asked as Merry slapped her chubby palms on the table.

"Two people connected to Kris who are now missing," Fern said, holding up two fingers. "First, Jeannie who said that Kris was nervous because he saw something suspicious, and now Stanley, who was the first person to find the bloody suit."

"We don't know they're *missing* missing," Mack said, his voice quivering.

"Maybe you don't," Fern said, shivering and making the sign of the cross over his chest, "but I have a strong premonition that they're both in trouble."

"He's dressed up as a priest one too many times," I whispered to Reese.

"Agreed," my fiancé said, his voice low so only I could hear him. "But, for once, I agree with your dramatic friend. I have a bad feeling that there's more to this whole mess than we know."

CHAPTER 11

"**W**here have you been?" Richard's head popped over the divider between my living room and kitchen as Reese and I walked into the apartment. "Didn't you get my texts?"

I dug my phone out from the bottom of my purse, cringing when I saw that my ringer had been off and the screen was filled with Richard's messages, which were punctuated with significantly more exclamation points and question marks as I scrolled down. "Sorry. We were preoccupied."

Richard's head disappeared into the kitchen with him mumbling something I was glad I couldn't hear, as his tiny black-and-brown dog scampered over to us, sniffing our legs and yipping happily.

I was surprised to see that our apartment had been returned to its usual state, and impressed that Richard had packed up every linen, plate, and fork. Even the plastic glass racks were gone, which meant that some unhappy delivery guys had carried everything down three flights of stairs. The chic and uncomfortable furniture had vanished, and my old furniture was back in place, although the room did look a little frumpy in comparison to its earlier look. At least Richard had left the Christmas tree decorations up, so the overall look was festively frumpy.

Perfectly embodying the theme, Leatrice sat on the yellow twill couch in a green sweatshirt printed with a fake pointy collar and wide, red belt to make it look like she was an elf. The green cap on her head, however, was genuine, and the bells jingled as she moved.

"What are you doing here, Leatrice?" I asked, hoping I didn't sound unhappy to find her parked in my living room. "I thought you'd be with your hubby."

Since her wedding over the summer, Leatrice and Sidney Allen had become even more inseparable, which meant I saw much more of the quirky entertainment diva, but it also meant that my nosy neighbor spent much less time poking into my life. It was a trade-off I'd take any day of the week.

"Returning Hermès," she said. "Besides, my love muffin has a party tonight. A troupe of sugar plum fairies down at the Willard Hotel. I thought I'd see what you were up to."

Richard's head reappeared over the divider. "I told her we were insanely busy."

"Hey, Hermès." Reese leaned down and rubbed the dog's furry head. "Your daddy doesn't seem to have calmed down much."

"I heard that," Richard called out. "How could I have calmed down when you abandoned me for hours to do everything solo?"

"Hey!" Kate leaned out from the office down the hall. "You weren't solo, and you also didn't do that much work, unless you consider chopping food work."

"Actually, I do," Richard said, "and so do my many cooks and pantry staff." He waved a wooden spoon in my direction. "You know cooking calms me, darling, and with everything going on, I thought I'd whip up a little grouper with tarragon shallot cream sauce to help me think."

Some people used meditation apps or miniature sand gardens to calm them. Richard cooked.

"Well, it smells amazing." Reese headed for the kitchen. "I was expecting to order takeout for dinner."

Richard shot me a look. "Please tell me that you and Annabelle do more than order takeout every night."

"We do," I said. Sometimes we went out to eat, and sometimes we ate cereal on the couch.

"Good news." Kate walked down the hall waving her phone. "I just heard back from Autoshop."

"Is your car in the shop?" Reese asked. "Brakes again?"

Kate was unquestionably a horrible driver, and slammed on her brakes so often when driving around downtown DC that she went through brake pads like some people went through paper towels.

"No." Kate laughed. "Autoshop is an event venue down at Union Market."

"It used to be an actual auto body shop, so it's got a cool industrial vibe, and has been completely refurbished," I told him then turned to Kate. "I can't believe they're available on New Year's Eve."

"Cancellation," Kate said. "We got lucky. How did it go with Jeannie?"

"Not so lucky." I saw my fiancé's brow crease. "Jeannie hasn't shown up at her usual place today."

"Do you think she heard about Kris's bloody Santa suit and wanted to be alone?" Kate asked.

"I might think that if she hadn't disappeared before the suit was found," I said. "And then the homeless guy who was one of the ones who found the suit was gone when we went to find him at Lush."

Kate put one hand on her hip. "That's weird."

"Did you say bloody Santa suit?" Leatrice moved faster than any eighty-year-old I'd ever met and was standing next to us in mere seconds, bouncing up and down on her toes.

"Oh, no." Richard joined us, pointing his wooden spoon at each of us. "I know exactly where this is headed, and I won't have it."

"What are you talking--?" I began, but Richard silenced me with a flourish of his spoon.

"Don't play coy with me, Annabelle. You know perfectly well what I mean. First it starts with a seemingly innocent discussion of the case, then it moves to someone thinking it sounds suspicious, and before you know it we're running amateur sting operations and running for our lives from deranged murderers." He heaved in a breath, his face red. "I'm telling you right now, we barely have time to pull off these weddings and your engagement party. There is no room in our lives for a murder investigation."

"Murder?" Leatrice's eyes danced. "I was wondering when you'd get another one."

"There's no murder," I said, although I didn't have high hopes the police would find Kris alive considering how much blood he--or someone--had lost.

Richard swung his spoon around, nearly whacking her in the elf cap. "Exactly. There is not, I repeat not, 'another one'."

"Of course not, dear," she said. "You seem very agitated. Do you need to lie down for a second?"

"If I'm agitated, it's only because Miss Marple here can't seem to stop meddling in investigations."

"If you remember," I said, "I was the one who insisted that we didn't have time when Fern first mentioned that Kris was missing."

Richard glared at me and ignored Leatrice. "It always seems to start out that way, and then you slowly get sucked in. You can't resist the urge to fix things. You never have. Mark my words, this case will be just like the others. You hunting for clues while you pretend you aren't, all of us ending up in danger, and me a nervous wreck."

That did sum up the last few criminal investigations we'd been involved in.

Reese put a hand on Richard's shoulder. "Now you know how I feel."

Richard sighed. "She used to be much worse, you know."

"Hello?" I waved my hands. "I'm standing right here."

My fiancé steered Richard back into the kitchen where I could hear them commiserating about how stubborn I was. I was sincerely regretting all the effort I'd put into getting them to be friends. Apparently, I'd done *too* good of a job.

Leatrice tugged me by the sleeve back toward the couch. "Where did you find the victim?"

"There is no victim," I said, keeping my voice low. "It was just his Santa suit covered in blood."

Leatrice tilted her head, and her bells jingled as the cap slid down her jet-black hair. "So you don't know if Kris Kringle Jingle is dead or not?"

I shook my head. "We're hoping he abandoned his suit, but there was a lot of blood."

"Who would want to hurt a man who dressed up like Santa and made people happy?" Leatrice asked.

"Well, according to some of his friends, not everyone was happy with all the attention he got, especially the bell-ringing Santas." I glanced toward the kitchen. "And Richard's right. This Santa turf war —if that's what it is—is one case we need to leave to the police. We have our hands full as it is."

"So are you going to tell Richard or let him twist in the wind a little longer?" Kate asked.

"Definitely twist," I said with a grin.

Kate grabbed her pink purse from the overstuffed chair and slung it over her shoulder. "As much as I'd like to watch him spiral out of control, I have a date tonight."

"A date?" Leatrice rubbed her palms together. "Tell me about your young man."

"Well, for one, he isn't all that young."

"You're going out with the older guy?" I asked, my interest immediately piqued. "I thought you weren't going out with him because you didn't want to settle down."

She held up both palms. "It's just a date. We're not hitting a wedding chapel after dinner." She pulled out her car keys. "You want me to pick you up tomorrow morning?"

"Tomorrow morning?" I thought for a moment before snapping my fingers. "Delivering our icicle-themed gift bags to the hotels in eighty-degree weather. Yes, pick me up. I have a really great parking space I don't want to lose."

"Have fun, dearie." Leatrice waved as Kate walked out, closing the front door behind her.

Reese emerged from the kitchen and gave me two thumbs up, which I took to mean that he'd calmed down Richard.

"Dinner will be ready in five minutes," Richard called out, confirming my assumption with his chirpy tone.

I walked over and took my fiancé's hand. "You're the Richard Whisperer."

"If only that was a paid position," he said with a wicked grin. "I feel like I could pull in a decent amount of overtime."

My phone vibrated in my hand and I glanced down at it, surprised to see Kate's name pop up. "Second thoughts about the date?" I joked when I answered.

"No," she said. "But I won't be able to pick you up tomorrow morning after all."

"Why not?"

Kate exhaled loudly. "Because someone flattened all my tires."

CHAPTER 12

"Can you believe that?" I asked Reese after we'd returned back upstairs from waiting with Kate for a tow truck. We'd deposited Leatrice in her first-floor apartment just in time for an episode of *Matlock,* and I was looking forward to some quiet time with my fiancé.

"What's not to believe?" Richard asked, walking out from the kitchen holding a plate in each oven-mitted hand. "Potential murder? Sabotage? Just another day in the life of Wedding Belles."

I exchanged a look with Reese. From his expression, I suspected it had slipped his mind that Richard was waiting with dinner.

Richard hesitated when he saw us staring at him. "What? You don't think I'm going to let this perfectly lovely sauce go to waste, do you? Even if you did take so long the fish could now be mistaken for high-end jerky."

"It still smells great," I said, in an attempt to mask my surprise.

Richard put the plates on my dining table, which was devoid of the elaborate decor from earlier. The handblown crystal had been replaced by my basic wine glasses; the eight pieces of sterling silver flatware per plate had been pared down to my stainless steel knives and forks, and instead of silk napkins in gilded napkin rings, there were plain plaid napkins folded in rectangles. The only reminder that there had been a photo shoot was the colorful floral arrangement that stretched down the middle and gave off the faint scent of lilies.

"I suppose you got Kate off to her date and her car off to the shop?" he asked, oven mitts on his hips. He seemed oddly calm about the whole thing, which made me nervous.

I nodded. "She was late for her date and pretty upset about having to get four new tires, but her car should be ready some time tomorrow."

Richard spun around and headed back to the kitchen, talking over his shoulder. "Any idea who did the deed, detective?"

"No clues that would pinpoint who did it," Reese said. "Definitely intentional, though. It looked like a sharp object--like a screwdriver-- was used to poke a hole in each tire."

"I wouldn't have been surprised if Kate had popped one tire, considering how many curbs she runs up onto and potholes she nails, but even she couldn't have hit four all at once," I said. "This was definitely the work of Brianna."

My fiancé put an arm around me. "You can't know that for sure, babe. No one saw her, and the only CCTV camera pointed in the direction of Kate's parked car is the one at the store across the street, and the manager said it wasn't recording."

I felt a fresh wave of frustration that I'd lost the chance to have a recording of our arch nemesis Brianna committing a crime. "Why have a camera if you don't turn it on?"

"Deterrence," Reese said, giving me a squeeze.

Richard returned carrying a final plate. "Speaking of deterrence, I don't suppose this little incident has convinced you to leave well enough alone?"

"This had nothing to do with the investigation into Kris Kringle Jingle's disappearance," I said. "This is 100 percent Brianna. She's the one who called me and made the threat, and she's the one who popped Kate's tires."

Richard shrugged as he set the final plate on the table and whipped off the oven mitts. "Maybe. Maybe not. You can't tell me it's another wild coincidence that someone goes missing at the same time you and Kate are sent a very clear message."

"Of course I can. The message is don't work with brides who fire Brianna. If I followed your logic, we shouldn't have taken the New Year's Eve wedding, which we are now in the position to ask you to cater. You still think I should leave well enough alone? Maybe tell the client to find someone else? Another planner who doesn't use Richard Gerard Catering, perhaps?"

Richard's mouth dangled open. "I hadn't thought of it from that angle." He sniffed and smoothed down the front of his apron. "You know I'd never advise you to abandon a client, darling."

I gave him a pointed look. "What about the threats and sabotage?"

He straightened his shoulders. "We must soldier on, of course. We can't let some upstart like Brianna interfere in our work, especially when we only have a couple of weeks to pull it all together." He waved a hand at the table. "Sit, sit. I'll get the wine."

"Well played," Reese whispered as we took our seats at the table.

"I know his pressure points," I said, keeping my voice low. "He can't stand the thought of not being part of a big event. He might take a bullet himself if it means a big enough check and a magazine feature."

Richard returned with a bottle of cold Chardonnay, which he handed off to Reese. "You're absolutely sure the tire slasher couldn't have been connected to the Kris Kringle case?"

"How could they be?" I asked as my fiancé poured the wine. "Kate hasn't been involved so far and neither has her car. But Brianna knows the kind of car Kate drives, and she made a threat. Besides, we don't know what happened to Kris."

"Whatever it was, it wasn't good," muttered Richard.

I sighed with a bite of fish halfway to my mouth. He was right about that. "So there's no proof Brianna popped Kate's tires, and we don't know who killed Kris or why."

Reese raised an eyebrow and swallowed a mouthful. "We?"

"Yes, Annabelle." In Richard's case, both eyebrows were raised. "What do you mean we?"

"Nothing," I said, focusing on my plate.

Reese put one hand over mine. "Why don't we make a deal? I know you're physically incapable of letting things go." He held up a hand when I started to protest. "Babe, I know you. You can't *not* try to fix things. It's in your DNA. It's one of the maddeningly charming things I love about you."

"Maddening is right," Richard mumbled, ignoring the look I shot him.

"If I promise to keep you looped into the case the entire way--which I'm not supposed to be doing with a civilian, by the way--will you promise not to interfere?" Reese asked.

"You'd have better luck tying her up and keeping her in a closet until you've found Kris," Richard said, again avoiding my eyes.

"I can do that," I said, shooting daggers at Richard and smiling sweetly at my fiancé. "As long as I can tell Fern and Buster and Mack that you're doing everything you can to find Kris."

"Trust me, babe. I want to find him alive as much as anyone. He's a Georgetown institution. The holidays aren't going to feel the same without him."

My throat tightened, and I reached for my wine. "If the temperature doesn't drop, it will feel like Christmas in the Sahara."

A few file folders sat stacked by Richard's plate, and he tapped them with a finger. "Speaking of our unfortunately themed wedding this weekend, I know I'm only doing the rehearsal dinner," he let out a tortured sigh, "but I'm going to have to rework this après ski motif."

"You know I can't stop clients from having hotel weddings," I said, for the umpteenth time. "The bride's family loves the Four Seasons. Just be glad I talked them out of having the entire weekend there. Plus, their rehearsal dinner is more elaborate than some weddings."

"Yes, but it isn't the event that gets top billing, is it?"

I shook my head. "When you say rework, what do you mean? The menu cards are already printed."

"I've resigned myself to the ridiculousness of our cheese fondue station and apple cider shooters in eighty-degree weather, but I cannot have my waiters walking around in alpine sweaters. I know it was my idea to make them look more festive, but that was when I thought it would be chilly. Now we're going to be able to use the outdoor space, and I do not want waiters dropping from heatstroke in December."

"That's fine," I said. "Have them wear tuxes."

Richard made a face. "I'm sure I can come up with something a bit more special than tuxedos, darling."

"I still have to decide if we should scrap the hot cocoa station at the valet station on Saturday night," I said. "We already have the cardboard cuffs for the to-go cups embossed with icicles, but I can't imagine people will be lining up for a hot drink when it feels like summer."

"Put it inside and crank up the AC," Reese said. "Can't you get a fake snow machine to pump out some snow? People would go for it if they got snowed on at the same time."

Richard gaped at him. "You know, that's not a bad idea." He nudged me. "You didn't tell me he has an instinct for events."

"Detectives do have problem-solving skills," Reese said.

I noticed Richard studying my fiancé and leveled a finger at him. "Don't even think about it."

"What?" Richard widened his eyes and attempted to look innocent.

"You know what," I told him. "You're scheming to think of ways you can put him to work for you."

"Nonsense," Richard said. "But if he happens to be around when we discuss our events, far be it from me to stop him from sharing his ideas."

"Be careful you don't end up on his payroll," I said to Reese. "Or serving apple cider shooters in an alpine sweater."

"Don't be silly, darling." Richard laughed, before cutting his eyes to Reese. "Although he would look good in a sweater, and you know I like my servers to be attractive."

Reese had ping-ponged his head back and forth without saying a word. Finally, he swallowed and shook his head. "I appreciate the vote of confidence, but I'm happy on the force, and frankly, I think it's less stressful than wedding planning or catering."

"Isn't that the truth?" Richard said, draining his glass of wine.

My fiancé's phone buzzed, and he pulled it out of his pants pocket, looking down at the screen and frowning. "Hobbes just responded to an anonymous call and found an apartment filled with stolen electronics."

I swallowed a bite and dabbed my lips with my napkin. "That's a good thing, right?"

"Sure." Reese absently scratched the stubble on his chin. "But the guys who apparently lived there and stole everything were tied up with Christmas tree garland and wearing Santa hats."

Richard raised his wine glass. "I've said it before and I'll say it again, the holidays make people crazy."

CHAPTER 13

"That was the third bellman that's laughed at our welcome bags," Kate said as she slid into the passenger seat of my car. I'd idled in front of the Georgetown Inn with my flashers on while she'd run inside the redbrick hotel with two armloads of ice-blue bags embossed with shiny silver icicles. Even the tissue paper was iridescent silver and the name tags were white snowflakes.

"Ignore them," I said, turning off my flashers and pulling back into traffic. "How could we know we'd get a heat wave when we ordered everything?"

Kate swiped a hand across her forehead and leaned one arm out the window. "Heat wave is right. This is ridiculous. I was so excited for boot weather, and I really should be pulling out my flip-flops."

I couldn't argue with her as I let the breeze from the open car window hit my face. I was wearing a sleeveless red plaid dress I usually paired with a turtleneck, but now wore solo. "We can only hope the weather turns, and everyone who laughed at us will be eating crow."

"Fried crow," Kate said under her breath as she fanned herself. "You know, I much prefer being the wheelman than being the delivery girl."

"Sorry," I said, although I was not sorry Kate wasn't behind the wheel of my car. "Any word on the new tires?"

"What's there to say about tires, except for the fact that they're now my Christmas gift to myself?" She shook her head. "I can't believe Reese couldn't fingerprint the ones that were popped."

"I doubt the person touched them when they did it," I said. "Plus, if Brianna did do it, I don't think she's in the system."

Kate snorted. "Don't be so sure." She glanced over at me as I headed out of Georgetown, passing the harbor and going underneath the highway. "Where are we going now? We're out of welcome bags and hotels to deliver them to."

I stopped at the red light at the top of K Street. "Autoshop. I thought we should do a walk-through before we have the clients sign the contract."

"So we're actually spending the whole day doing wedding work?" Kate gave me an approving look as she nodded slowly. "I'm a little surprised."

"What else would we be doing?" I asked, gunning the engine as the light turned green.

"Oh, I don't know. Poking around in your fiancé's case, organizing a secret search party for Kris Kringle Jingle, having Leatrice hack into the police computers to check on the case's progress. You know, the usual."

"Very funny." I breathed in the smell of exhaust and food trucks as we headed down K Street. "Even if I did want to do those things, I've been threatened under pain of death by Richard. Reese and his guys are still searching for Kris and questioning the Salvation Army bell ringers, and he promised to let me know as soon as they find anything, although he's now also working on the case of the burglars who were tied up and wearing Santa hats."

"That is weird, but I'll bet some of their criminal buddies turned them in and decided to get creative with it. There's no honor among thieves, but there might be a sense of humor."

"At least it closes some of the robbery cases Reese was working on. Apparently, the thieves had hit a bunch of Georgetown houses in the past month."

"So now they're trying to find out who turned them in?" Kate asked.

"Yes, but more to thank whomever did it. Reese is still focused on finding Kris."

"What do you think the chances are they're going to find him alive?" Kate asked.

"You never know. As long as they don't have a body, there's a chance he survived whatever happened to him." I repeated Reese's words, although I suspected I believed them about as much as he did.

"It's pretty weird there was no body. I mean, we've been involved in more than our fair share of murder investigations, and never have we just found bloody clothes."

She made a good point.

I drummed my fingers against the steering wheel. "Which means there's a chance it wasn't a murder and Kris ditched the Santa suit after being wounded."

"Or someone took it off him and dumped the body where it wouldn't be found," Kate said.

A less pleasant option.

"Either way," I said, "Reese is on the case. Not to mention Buster and Mack and their homeless crew. When we left them yesterday, they were heading out to sweep the area again. If anyone knows places to stash a body, it's the people who know the streets."

"Although if it was another homeless person or Salvation Army Santa, they'd know all the spots, too."

"Hmm." I hadn't thought about that. Our only suspects were other people who knew the streets.

Kate gave me a side-eye look. "I'm glad to see you taking a back seat on this one. If you really want to solve something, you should focus on proving that Brianna popped my tires."

I entered a busy traffic circle and exited onto Massachusetts Avenue. "We both know it was her even if we can't prove it. Who else would do something like that?"

Kate held her hands palm up. "And what did I ever do to her?"

I cut my eyes to my assistant. "You mean, aside from spread the rumor that her business is a front for a prostitution ring?"

She shook a finger at me. "I only did that after she told everyone that we were murder magnets."

To be fair, saying we were murder magnets wasn't totally off base. It wasn't nice, but it wasn't completely wrong.

"I'm not thrilled that she's escalated from trash talking to vandalism," I said. "But she seems to think everything we do is a personal attack on her."

"We didn't even know she was the planner the New Year's Eve client had fired," Kate said. "Maybe she should focus on being a better planner instead of lashing out at the rest of us."

"I wonder if they have a greeting card for that."

"A greeting card is not what I was thinking of sending her," Kate muttered. "More like the bill for my tires."

I was glad it was December, and Kate would be getting her holiday bonus from me soon. After last night, I knew what it would be going toward. "Are we doing a holiday party for the gang this year? I know it's kind of crazy right now, but we always do something."

Kate twisted in her seat to face me. "I meant to ask you, how do you feel about combining your engagement party with the Wedding Belles holiday party?"

"Since I wasn't the one who wanted an engagement party in the first place, I'm fine with anything." I smiled at the idea. "Actually, I think it's great. It will make it less like an engagement party."

Kate let out a long breath. "You have to have an engagement party, Annabelle. You're a wedding planner. This is your business. How are we supposed to convince our clients they need all these fabulous things for their weddings if you and Reese run off to the courthouse?"

"We're hardly running off to the courthouse," I said, sighing almost as loudly as she had. "We just haven't had time to focus on planning yet."

"Which is why I took over and became your official wedding planner, but it would be helpful to get some feedback." She held up two fingers. "I'm this close to booking bride and groom llamas for your cocktail hour."

I laughed. "You know how Richard gets about livestock at events. I do not want to see him running around with a pooper scooper and rubber gloves again."

"Okay, that's a no on the llamas."

"But a yes to the holiday party/engagement party mash-up," I reminded her. "Most of our guests would have been at both anyway. The only difference this time will be the addition of Reese's cop buddies. It will be like a Wedding Belles holiday party that's being raided."

Kate snapped her fingers. "And there's our theme!"

Before I could tell her the many reasons why that was not a great engagement party theme, I spotted a woman with a long white braid hurrying across the street, an overstuffed IKEA bag hanging off one shoulder. She disappeared into a brick building with large wooden doors.

I grabbed my phone from the center console and pressed one of my pre-programmed speed dial numbers.

"Annabelle, what a lovely surprise," Fern said when he answered.

"Quick question," I said. "What color hair does Jeannie have?"

"Jeannie? White. It's quite pretty, although it would look even better if she let me cut it and give her layers, but she's about as open to change with her hair as you are, sweetie. Why do you ask?"

"I'm assuming she didn't show up for her wash and style this morning?" I answered his question with one of my own.

"How did you know?"

I jerked my car to the curb in front of the building the woman had run into. "Because I'm pretty sure I just saw her halfway across town."

CHAPTER 14

"Whoa," Kate said as I hopped out of the car. "Where are you going? What happened to our site visit?"

I hitched my purse over my shoulder and looked up at the three-story brick building with tall windows lined up in a grid. "I just want to pop in here and see if the woman I saw was actually Jeannie."

Kate jumped out of the car on her side, slamming the door as she followed me. "I thought we weren't going to get involved with the case. I thought we were laser focused on our events."

I paused to let her catch up to me in her highheeled mules. "This isn't getting involved. This is doing a favor for Fern."

"Really?" Kate muttered as she wobbled up the steps toward the large double doors with an imposing brick and stone archway overhead that read "Gales School." "Because this feels an awful lot like getting involved."

I put a hand on the metal door handle as I read the sign printed on the glass--"Central Union Mission." "You know Fern is worried sick about Kris and Jeannie. If we can tell him that one of them is safe, wouldn't that be a good thing?"

"I feel like you're sneaking this through on a technicality,

Annabelle, but I'll let it slide. But only if this is an in-and-out operation. If we end up cowering in a storage closet or rummaging through
someone's office for evidence, I'm out of here, *and* I'm telling Richard."

I exhaled, shaking my head. "Since when are you on his side?"

"Since his side became the one where I don't get nearly arrested."

"Fine, but I'm telling you, this is perfectly innocent." I peered
through the glass top of the doors, seeing another set of doors and a
wide hallway beyond that. "We look for Jeannie, maybe talk with her,
and then we leave."

"So you say." She yanked open one of the doors and held it open
for me.

"When did you become the voice of reason?" I asked, grinning
at her.

We walked inside, passing through the second set of double doors
and pausing. Although the outside of the building indicated the
shelter had been a school in its former life, the inside had a long, well-
lit hallway and the walls looked freshly painted, even if the paint
choice was a gray on gray. I smelled food and realized it must be
around lunchtime as people disappeared through a doorway to the
right. I didn't know if the mission was a residential shelter or if it only
provided meals and services, but it seemed to be bustling.

"Do I smell fried chicken?" Kate asked, sucking in a deep breath.

"Since when do you eat fried food?"

She inhaled again. "I don't, but I love to smell it."

I rolled my eyes, motioning for Kate to follow me as I peeked my
head into the well-trafficked doorway.

The room had windows along one side and long fluorescent lights
in the ceiling, with tables and attached benches stretching the width of
the space. In the corner was an entrance to a kitchen and what
appeared to be a buffet line and stacks of green trays.

Kate nudged me. "Is that her?"

I followed her line of sight and spotted the woman with the white
braid down her back. "She matches Fern's description."

Kate tapped her wrist, even though she didn't wear a watch. "Then
let's do this and get out of here. Autoshop is waiting."

I wound my way to where the woman sat with her back to us. She wasn't eating, but seemed to be nursing a Styrofoam cup of coffee. Walking around the table, I took a seat directly across from her.

She glanced up and her pale-blue eyes flickered something-- concern, fear, confusion? "Who are you?"

"We're friends of Fern's," I said.

She sized us both up as Kate sat next to me. "That makes sense." She motioned her head toward Kate. "Especially her."

I tried not to take that as a passive-aggressive comment about my messy ponytail. "You're Jeannie, right?"

She nodded and took a sip of coffee.

"He's worried about you," I said, when I realized she wasn't much of a talker. "You missed your usual appointment this morning."

Her eyes darted around the room, then dropped to her cup. "Can you tell him I'm sorry about that?"

"He'd rather hear it from you," Kate said. "You know how Fern worries."

Jeannie let out a small laugh. "That man sure is a mess of nerves."

A pretty accurate assessment. When she didn't say more, I continued. "And the folks at Clyde's are worried, too."

She shifted on the bench. "Can you tell them I needed a few days off? I'll be back soon."

I leaned closer. "Why do you need a few days off? Is this about Kris?"

Her head jerked up. "Are you here about him?"

"No," I said. "We're here because Fern was worried about you, but everyone is pretty concerned about Kris, too. You heard they found his Santa suit, right?"

Jeannie pressed her lips together and nodded.

"I know you told my fiancé that Kris was worried about something before he disappeared. Something he saw. Do you think that could have gotten him killed?"

She eyed me warily. "Your fiancé? You mean that good-looking cop Fern brought around? You're engaged to him?"

I tried not to be offended for the second time in the conversation. "Yes, he's my fiancé."

"She looks a lot better when she tries," Kate said. "You should have seen her yesterday. She had fake lashes and everything."

Jeannie cocked an eyebrow at me as if she was trying to imagine me with false eyelashes.

I sighed. "Back to Kris. Did he seem to be afraid for his life?"

Jeannie dropped her gaze back to her cup and shrugged. "He seemed concerned, but Kris doesn't like to let anything upset him too much. He says he can't sing if he's in a bad mood."

"And you don't know of anyone who would want him dead?" I asked. "Or what he saw?"

She shook her head sharply. "Everyone loves Kris."

"Not everyone," I said. "We heard that some of the bell ringers weren't crazy about him, and even some of your homeless friends didn't like his policy of not taking money."

Jeannie looked over her shoulder and dropped her voice. "Those Salvation Army Santas can get real competitive. It's not a big secret they don't like Kris, but kill him?" She shook her head. "And none of our people would do that either. Even if they didn't like his singing shtick. It had to be someone else."

It seemed to be the general consensus that no one would have hurt Kris, but clearly *someone* did. A man sat next to me, the smell of fried chicken and macaroni and cheese wafting up from his plate. My stomach growled, reminding me of my banana and coffee breakfast.

"So if it wasn't an angry Santa trying to knock off the competition, what about what he saw? He didn't tell you anything more about it?"

Another shake of her head. "Just that they shouldn't be doing that sort of thing around the holidays." The corner of her mouth quirked up. "He's touchy about people messing with Christmas."

I guess that made sense. He did dress up like Santa and sing carols just to make people happy, so he had a certain claim to the holly jolly holiday.

"And he didn't want to go to the cops about it?" I asked.

Jeannie shrugged.

I wondered if he thought he wouldn't be taken seriously because he was homeless or because he dressed up like Santa and sang carols. None of us said anything for a few minutes.

"This seems like a nice place," Kate finally said, swiveling her head around. "The food smells good."

Jeannie nodded and took another tiny sip of coffee.

I twisted my head to take in the quickly filling dining room, as well. "It's not all that close to Georgetown, though."

"I like to move around," she said.

I nodded but knew that contradicted everything Fern had told me about the woman. She was a Georgetown institution, much like Kris Kringle Jingle. I looked at the tight set of her jaw and the thin line of her mouth. No way was this woman going to talk to us, even if she knew something. I suspected her being halfway across town—and the nervous way she scanned the room—had something to do with Kris. Was she avoiding Georgetown because, despite what she said, she considered one of the other homeless there a threat? Was she avoiding being seen by a murderous bell ringer? Was she afraid that her connection with Kris put her in danger? Whatever the reason, the expression on her face told me she wasn't going to tell us.

I stood. "My fiancé is determined to find out what happened to your friend. The forensics unit is inspecting the recovered Santa suit for clues, so hopefully we'll have more information soon."

Her head snapped up, her brows pressed together forming a hard crease between her eyes. "They can know things just from that bloody suit?"

"Sure," I said. "Forensics is pretty impressive."

Kate stood next to me. "But don't think it's like CSI. None of the forensic techs are even remotely as hot in real life."

I didn't want to know how my assistant knew the "hotness" of the DC forensics department.

"Thanks for talking to us," I said. "We'll tell Fern and the folks at Clyde's you're okay."

Jeannie gnawed on her bottom lip. "Tell that cute cop of yours thanks from me. Not everyone takes us seriously, but he didn't look at me like I was crazy when Fern brought him around and told him about Kris."

"Of course he didn't think you were crazy," Kate said. "He's friends with Fern."

That got a small smile from Jeannie. "Sometimes I think that one might be a sandwich short of a picnic."

"Most creative geniuses are," I said.

"Which explains the entire wedding industry," Kate said under her breath as we left Jeannie.

When we'd gotten outside, I looked over my shoulder. "I'm glad she's okay."

"Too bad she didn't tell us anything."

I let Kate hang onto my arm as we walked down the concrete steps. "What do you mean? She gave us a huge clue."

"Just now?" Kate glanced back at the building. "Was she talking in code?"

I shrugged. "She told us that Kris isn't dead."

"She did?"

"Didn't you notice how she referred to him in the present tense? Most people have assumed he's dead when they hear his suit was found soaked in blood, but she didn't seem all that concerned and she talked about him as if she knows he's alive."

"Maybe she's an optimist," Kate suggested, opening her side of the car and leaning against the top of the doorframe.

"Or maybe she knows something we don't." I nibbled the corner of my lip as we both got into the car. "I hope she isn't in danger."

"Either way, I wouldn't worry about her too much."

I cut my eyes to Kate as I started the car and eased it into traffic. "What happened to your Christmas spirit?"

She shook her head and jerked a thumb behind her. "I mean, I wouldn't worry because it looked like the cops were keeping an eye on her."

"The cops?" I craned my neck around quickly, but we were already a block away.

"Didn't you notice the two guys in the unmarked car parked a few spaces in front of us?"

I hadn't. "How do you know they were cops?"

Kate gave me a withering look. "Have I ever been wrong about predicting a man's profession by his clothing?" She didn't wait for me to answer. "Trust me, they were cops."

So someone in the police department was keeping an eye on Jeannie, but my fiancé clearly had no idea. This got more interesting—and baffling—by the second.

CHAPTER 15

"So are we back to wedding business?" Kate asked as we walked up the metal stairs leading into Autoshop.

I dropped my phone back into my purse. "Absolutely. Fern is happy to hear that Jeannie is okay, and I told Reese so he wouldn't worry about searching for her as well as Kris. Now if we only knew what happened to the homeless man who found the Santa suit."

Kate paused at the wide entrance to the long room with exposed brick walls and steel beams running along the ceiling. "But in a detached curiosity way, right?"

"Of course. I promise to be completely focused on our walk-through." I scanned the space, which was the embodiment of indus-trial chic and made me feel like I should be wearing hipster glasses and have the tips of my hair dyed pink.

"Good, because we don't have long to figure out a design plan for the space," Kate said. "But don't you think it's perfect?"

"It *is* a blank slate." I stepped into the room, my shoes tapping on the concrete floors, and gazed down at the tall windows that ran across the far end of the space. "We could do just about anything with it."

"Exactly." Kate walked into the middle of the empty room and spread her arms out wide. "Since the bride wants a time theme, we could hang clocks from the ceiling over each table."

I turned to look at the rough, redbrick walls as my mind raced with ideas. "I wonder if we could rent grandfather clocks to position along the walls."

"And look at this elevated space we could use for cocktails." Kate strode to the other side of the room where more black metal stairs led to a long, narrow space that ran parallel to the main room and had whitewashed brick walls.

I followed her up the stairs until we were standing in the cocktail space, which featured more large windows and doors to an outdoor terrace. "We could put two bars against the walls inside and maybe another outside."

Kate snapped her fingers. "That reminds me. I need to think up a name for our specialty cocktail."

"This wedding is having a specialty cocktail?" I asked.

"Annabelle." She patted my hand. "All weddings should have a specialty cocktail."

"You've really drunk the Instagram Kool-Aid, haven't you?"

"For the right party, *that* could be a cute name for a custom cocktail," she said, winking at me. "But for a time-themed New Year's Eve wedding, I was thinking about the Melon Ball Drop or the Thyme After Thyme with actual thyme sprigs for garnish."

"Cute," I admitted. "How long have you been brainstorming those?"

Kate grinned. "Since the bride signed the contract."

I crossed to one of the windows overlooking the terrace and spotted the top of the Capitol in the distance. "Normally, I wouldn't think a terrace would be very useful for a New Year's Eve wedding, but this year we could actually use it."

"Don't remind me." Kate slipped on her oversized sunglasses as sunlight streamed through the windows. "I hate sweating in December."

"At least this wedding isn't stuck with a snowflake theme," I said.

"You have got to be kidding me," Kate said as she slid her sunglasses to the end of her nose and squinted over them.

"I never kid about themes, Kate. You know that. Complain about them, yes. But kid..."

She elbowed me to cut me off. "It's the tire slasher."

"The what?" I watched as her face hardened into a scowl. "Wait. Do you mean Brianna?" I followed her gaze and saw the blond wedding planner flouncing into the event space from the other side. "What is she doing here?'

"Stalking us," Kate said, not taking her eyes off the woman.

I instinctively put a hand on Kate's arm. "You know you can't run over there and accuse her of slashing your tires."

"Why not?"

"Because then she'll know she's getting to us," I said. "The last thing we want is for someone like her to think she's winning."

"Good point." Kate took a deep breath. "Can I kick her? Accidentally?"

"No," I said. "Remember, revenge is a dish best served cold."

Kate made a face. "That doesn't make any sense. What tastes good cold? Are you sure you're saying it right?"

"Positive," I told her. "Now let's go make sure that two-bit tramp knows she isn't getting to us."

Kate grinned. "I love it when Fern rubs off on you."

We walked down from the cocktail area and crossed the room toward Brianna, who stood next to a pair of young women who looked like they could be in high school and were both engrossed in their phones. When the tall blond saw us, her smile froze and she muttered something under her breath that made both women's heads snap up.

"If it isn't the crime-fighting duo themselves," she said in her syrupy Southern accent, laughing at her own joke.

"What are you doing here?" Kate asked, putting her hands on her hips and rapping the toe of her shoe on the floor. "I know you don't have a wedding booked here."

"Styled shoot," one of the girls said. "At least that's what we're trying for."

Brianna's cheeks flushed pink, and she shot daggers at the girl.

"You're so lucky to have the time on your hands to do styled shoots," Kate said, her voice dripping with fake sincerity. "That's the problem with having so many paying clients, like our wedding at the Four Seasons this weekend and the Ritz last weekend. We barely have time to breathe, much less dream up fake events to photograph."

"That's because y'all are too busy stealing other planners' weddings," Brianna said, her eyes flashing.

Kate held up her hands. "We had nothing to do with the bride bailing on you. She didn't even call us until she'd fired you."

"She didn't tell us who her planner had been," I added. "We had no idea it was you."

Brianna glared at both of us. "Like I'd believe that. You've been trying to destroy me ever since I came here."

"Us?" Kate gaped at her. "You're the one who told everyone we were the wedding planners of death."

"Well, you are," Brianna practically screamed. "How many dead bodies have y'all found at your weddings? Ten? Twenty?"

The women with Brianna stared at us.

"Not twenty," I assured them, although I was fairly certain the number was higher than ten.

"Well, while you're running around like chickens with your heads cut off on New Year's Eve, I'm going to be hosting an industry party so over-the-top that no one will be talking about anything else for years." She wagged a finger at us. "Everyone will see just how much better a planner I am than you two."

"Listen, Brianna," I said, thinking that maybe our feud had gone on long enough. "That's silly. You don't need to spend a ton of money on a party to prove you're good."

"Silly?" She tossed her hair off her shoulder. "My daddy always says there isn't any problem that enough money can't fix."

I sighed. Someone wasn't going to win father of the year.

"I'm not sure how we got off on such a bad foot," I said, "but why don't we talk this out?"

"There's nothing to talk about." Brianna folded her arms tightly across her chest. "I'm sorry y'all are making me get ugly, but I'm done being sweet."

Kate folded her own arms. "This has been you being sweet?"

"Ladies," I said, making a last-ditch effort to diffuse the situation. "Let's all calm down."

"You call slashing my tires being sweet?" Kate asked, taking a step forward.

Both of Brianna's assistants swung their heads toward her, but she just smiled.

"Did your tires get slashed? Well, isn't that a shame?" She batted her eyelashes. "Maybe you made the wrong person angry."

"Maybe *you* did," Kate said, her voice menacing.

Brianna stepped back, clearing her throat. "I've had about enough of y'all threatening me."

Kate leaned forward, flicking her fingers at the three women. "Then I suggest you leave, sweetie."

Brianna spun on her heel and the other two women scurried after her, their shoes pattering as they hurried down the stairs.

"Well, that went well," I said.

"What?" Kate gave me her most innocent face. "I said 'sweetie'."

CHAPTER 16

"This is an odd way to go back to Georgetown," Kate said as I veered off Wisconsin Avenue and headed down Massachusetts Avenue.

Since it was still in the mid-seventies, I had my car windows down instead of cranking the AC. It just seemed wrong to use air conditioning in December, even if the weather called for it. I rested my arm on the window sill and breathed in. "We're not going back to Georgetown."

"Are we leaving the city to make our fortune elsewhere now that that crazy Brianna is after us?" Kate asked, reaching for the Blue Bottle coffee she'd gotten when we'd walked through the Union Market food stalls on our way out of Autoshop. "Because I'm okay with that plan. I think we could do well planning weddings on the beaches of Mexico."

"After we just pulled after a major coup and found a new wedding venue in a matter of days?"

"Good point," she said. "The bride was pretty thrilled just now when I told her the contract was in the works."

Kate had called the bride while I'd pulled the car around. Delivering good news to a client was something we never delayed.

She took a gulp of coffee. "But Mexico is never a bad option considering our track record."

I made a face at her. "Ha ha. We're not running off to Mexico. We're going to swing by the police station."

Kate took a sip from her to-go cup. "Is this your way of sneaking in some alone time with Reese?"

"No," I said, reaching for the blueberry lemonade I'd snagged from the Village Cafe, "but we're going to pretend it is."

"I'm confused."

"The guy who found Kris's Santa suit may be missing, but the cop who was with him isn't," I said, sipping my drink and puckering my lips at the tartness.

"So we're going to the police precinct your fiancé works at to see someone other than him?"

I made a right turn and slowed down as I entered a more residential street. "You got it."

"And when he catches us questioning a cop connected to the case, our excuse is going to be temporary insanity?"

"He won't catch us," I said. "He's supposed to be out looking for Kris."

"And we're supposed to be planning two weddings and an engagement party," Kate muttered.

I slowed down as we approached the square, two-story brick building that housed the police precinct, swinging my car nose first into a parallel spot on the street. "It's just a few questions. If I ask Reese, he'll think I'm trying to poke around in his case."

"Aren't you?" Kate took a final sip and placed her coffee back in the center console.

"Hardly." I opened my car door and stepped up onto the curb. "I'm trying to help him."

Kate got out and joined me on the sidewalk. "Explain."

"Kris's friend Jeannie was hiding something. Stanley, the only other witness of any kind, disappeared. If this case isn't what it seems, Reese could be wasting his time. The cop who was with Stanley might have some insight. I mean, he must know something or have some thoughts about why Stanley would have disappeared."

"So you're trying to prevent your fiancé from spinning his wheels?"

I pointed a finger at her. "Exactly. He's got his hands full with all the weird holiday-related crimes."

She nodded thoughtfully as we walked toward the dark glass front of the station. "Not bad. Not totally believable, but I've heard worse. What holiday-related crimes, aside from a singing Santa going missing?"

"Apparently there was a home invasion in upper Georgetown that went wrong late last night. The guy who was trying to break in ended up tied up with a holiday wreath shoved down around his waist. He was rolling around on the people's front porch when the cops arrived."

Kate gave a snort of laughter. "So the homeowners fought back? Good for them."

I pulled open one side of the tinted glass doors. "They insist it wasn't them. Said they heard scuffling and when they opened the door, the guy was struggling to get up, but couldn't because the wreath had his arms pinned down."

"So someone out there is helping the police catch bad guys? That's a good thing, right?"

I shrugged as Kate stepped into the building in front of me. "Technically, they aren't supposed to encourage citizens taking the law into their own hands, but I know Reese isn't complaining. He's been talking about crime in Georgetown being on the rise for a while now, as well as his suspicions that it's being run by a group and not just random perpetrators. I think he's grateful for any help in cracking the crime ring."

Kate hesitated. "You don't think my tire slashing was done by this crime ring, do you?"

I followed her inside, my shoes tapping on the dingy linoleum as we headed for the reception desk to the right. "From what Reese has told me, they don't do random vandalism."

"You're right. It has Brianna written all over it." She sucked in a breath, her face brightening. "Maybe Brianna is involved in the crime ring. Maybe she's actually a crime boss."

I raised an eyebrow at her. "Don't give her that much credit. She can't even plan a wedding properly. How would she run a criminal organization?"

"You make a good point." Kate winked at me. "That doesn't mean I can't spread the rumor that Brianna has gone from being a Madame to being a crime boss."

"That should help diffuse the situation," I said under my breath.

When we reached the faux wood desk, I smiled at the female officer standing behind it. My eyes flicked to the battered desks that extended behind the counter and the closed office doors at the far end. I saw a weathered coffee pot on a small table to one side with a trash can next to it filled to the rim with discarded sugar packets and plastic creamer pods. The building held the distinct scent of stale coffee and cigarette smoke, even though I knew you couldn't smoke inside.

"I'm Annabelle Archer," I said, keeping my smile wide as the woman leveled her gaze at me.

"She's engaged to Mike Reese," Kate added, leaning on the desk and flashing the woman, and the entire office, her cleavage. "Detective Mike Reese."

The female cop glanced at me, gave me the once-over, and nodded. "He's not here."

"Shoot," I said, trying to sound disappointed. "By any chance is Officer Rogers available?"

"Rookie Rogers?" She looked over her shoulder. "Hey, Rogers. You available?"

A cop with wispy, sandy-brown hair and a round, baby face rose from a desk in the back. He walked forward, his look of confusion turning into a smile as he got closer and no doubt got a better look at Kate. The female cop rolled her eyes and stepped away.

"How can I help you, ladies?" he asked, his attention on Kate.

I darted a quick look to my assistant. After working together for so many years, I liked to think we had an unspoken shorthand.

She blinked at me. "What?"

Stifling a groan, I widened my own eyes, which I cut in the direction of the cop.

"Ah." Understanding crossed her face, and she nodded her head almost imperceptibly before bestowing one of her most alluring smiles on the young cop. "Aren't you the one who found the Santa suit?"

His own smile dimmed a bit. "How did you know that?"

Kate jerked a thumb at me. "She's engaged to Mike Reese."

"Oh." He sounded relieved as he looked quickly at me then back at Kate and her low-cut top. "Yep. That was me."

"It must have been shocking," Kate leaned closer, "to find a bloody Santa suit like that."

"Actually, I didn't find it. I came up on the homeless guy as he was pulling it out of the dumpster. As soon as I realized what it was, I took control of the evidence and called it in."

"I'll bet you took control," Kate said, winking at him.

The rookie cop's cheeks flushed pink, and I hoped he wouldn't pass out before we could finish questioning him. This was one drawback to using Kate's charms to extract information.

"What happened to the homeless guy?" I asked.

Officer Rogers pulled his gaze away from Kate and thought for a second. "Stanley? I took his statement, but he didn't have much to say. He saw the suit hanging out of the dumpster and pulled it out."

"Did he seem nervous or upset?"

"Both, I guess, but that wasn't a surprise since Stanley has some mental issues and he knew the victim," Rogers said, smoothing his thinning hair to one side.

"Victim?" Kate tilted her head at him. "How do you know Kris is dead if you only found the suit?"

Rogers shrugged. "I don't, but there was a lot of blood. No one loses that much blood and survives."

"Shouldn't there be a body?" I asked.

"Lots of things could have happened to the body." His voice took on a more authoritative tone. "It could have been thrown in the river or driven out of the city, or maybe we just haven't found it yet."

All of this was true, so why did I have such a hard time believing Kris was dead? Was it because I didn't want to believe it despite all hard evidence to the contrary? I nodded, but I wasn't convinced.

"Why?" Rogers asked. "Does Reese think the Santa is still alive?"

The officer's question jerked me out of my thoughts. "What? No, I didn't say that."

He exhaled, rubbing two fingers down the bridge of his nose. "I know a lot of folks in Georgetown liked the guy, but sometimes living on the streets can be dangerous. And the homeless community isn't always so friendly to each other."

That wasn't what Jeannie had told us, but then again, she wouldn't want to make her community look bad by saying they didn't get along.

Kate flipped her hair off her face. "In what way?"

Rogers puffed his chest out a bit. "They fight over stuff and the best spots. Just like any group of people."

"Do you know a lot of the homeless people in Georgetown?" I asked.

He nodded. "It's my beat, so I know most of them by name."

"So you knew Kris personally?"

Another nod. "He was a good guy. Never bothered people. Always stopped to talk to me." He dropped his eyes. "I'll miss the fella."

"And you don't have any leads on what might have happened?" Kate asked, her now voice less coquettish.

"Living on the streets isn't good for your health, but I got the feeling that Stanley either knew more than he wanted to say or that he was involved."

"You think Stanley might have killed him?" My voice rose and I saw a cop glance over, so I lowered it quickly. "I thought they were buddies."

"Most homicides happen between friends and family," he said. "Anyone who draws attention to themselves like Kris did was bound to have haters. They could have gotten into an argument that got out of hand. Who knows? We'd also gotten complaints from some of the bell ringers in Georgetown. They thought he was poaching their donations."

"But he didn't take money," I said.

Rogers raised his palms. "I know. They still complained. But I'm just guessing about all this. Kris might have just been at the wrong place at the wrong time."

Kate tugged on my arm and inclined her head to the back of the room. "Speaking of being in the wrong place."

Crap. My fiancé had emerged from one of the back offices. So much for him being out. I ducked down and pretended to tie my shoes, even though they had no laces.

"Thanks for talking with us," Kate said above me, her voice low. "We can keep this visit just between us, right? I'll bet a good-looking guy like you knows how to keep a girl's secret."

I could only imagine the looks she was giving him to make him agree so enthusiastically.

"Gotta run," Kate said, hunching over and pulling me with her as she blew a kiss over her shoulder. "I'll call you."

I didn't look back until we were outside and halfway to my car. "Do you think Reese saw us?"

"He's not out here scolding us, is he?" Kate asked, not slowing down until we'd reached the car.

We jumped inside, and I quickly pulled away from the curb, not breathing easily until the police station was in my rearview mirror. "Well, that was interesting."

Kate reached for her coffee. "If you say so."

"Officer Rogers seemed convinced that Kris is dead, but Jeannie seems to think he isn't." I took a long sip of my blueberry lemonade. "Obviously, one of them is wrong."

Kate kicked off her heels and stretched out her legs. "And even more obviously, you want to find out which one."

CHAPTER 17

I jumped when my phone trilled in my purse. Please don't be Reese, I thought, as I pulled it out. I was not ready to explain why Kate and I had been sneaking out of the police station, especially after I'd promised to stay out of his case.

Kate snapped her head to me. "You don't think that's him, do you? Driving to Mexico is still on the table, you know."

Pulling the phone from my purse, I glanced at the screen and let out a loud sigh. Not Reese. "We don't have to make a run for the border. It's Richard."

"I'm not sure if that's much better. Let's not take Mexico off the table just yet."

I answered, trying to sound as cheery--and innocent--as possible.

"Would you care to explain why all my caterer friends are getting requests for a sizable proposal for New Year's Eve, and I'm not?" Richard asked, before I'd finished saying hello.

My car's Bluetooth was acting up, so I held the phone against my ear with one shoulder while I drove. Not the safest thing, but safer than ignoring Richard's call. "Because the proposal request is coming from Brianna, and you're guilty by association."

"Not the worst association I've been a part of," Richard said with a sniff.

Kate and I had left the police station and were almost back in Georgetown, with my assistant scrolling through emails at a blinding pace, as I navigated the traffic down Constitution Avenue.

"Tell him he'd be better off working with us on New Year's Eve," Kate said. "Brianna is crazy."

"Did you hear that?" I asked Richard, pumping the brakes as a traffic light turned red and the BMW in front of me gunned it through.

"Of course she's crazy," Richard said. "She's one of those bottle blondes from the South who's sniffed too much bleach and bourbon, but she's the kind of crazy who has daddy's money to back her up. Do you know what she's asking for in these proposals?"

"No," I admitted, although I couldn't help being impressed by how quickly the woman had sent out feelers.

"Lobster, King crab legs, caviar, the works. She even wants her after midnight snacks to be Kobe beef sliders."

So it really would be a party the wedding industry would be talking about for years. "Like you said, she's got her daddy's money to pay for it."

Richard let out a deep sigh. "It's too bad I'm past the point of hitching my cart to a sugar daddy."

"And get rid of PJ?" I said. "No way. Not after we finally met him. Trust me, a sugar daddy is not the answer."

"Depends on the question." Kate glanced over at me. "Is this still about Brianna?"

I nodded slowly, without dropping the phone. "She's sparing no expense for her party."

Kate shrugged. "But who's going? All of our crew will be with us, and I know some other planners who have events, not to mention all the hotels. The only people who will be available to attend are the ones without a party on the biggest party night of the year."

"Which is usually us," I reminded her, since we rarely took weddings over the stretch between Christmas and New Year's Day. "And weren't you just complaining about working too much over the holidays?"

Kate winked at me. "A girl can change her mind, can't she?"

"Kate has a point," Richard said. "New Year's Eve is not the night to snag all the event people. She should have picked a random Thursday, like everyone else does."

Because our industry work week focused on the weekend, all of our networking events were held on weeknights. And if a wedding planner wanted to host a social event, they never picked a Friday or Saturday. Those dates were for people who worked regular nine-to-five jobs.

"If she'd picked a different night, she wouldn't have gotten to screw over our new client and her former bride," I said. "And perhaps more importantly, she wouldn't have gotten to screw over us."

"I hope she and her five guests have fun," Kate said under her breath.

I slowed down as I merged onto M Street and headed into George-town proper. "We're almost at my apartment. Can I call you later?"

"We still need to discuss the menu for our New Year's Eve event, Annabelle, although I don't suppose I need to worry about Brianna snatching up all the King crab legs?"

"No," I told him. "Crab has not come up with the bride, nor have Kobe beef sliders. Sorry."

"Tell him if he plays his card right, we might be able to swing a dessert station," Kate said.

"Be still, my beating heart," Richard drawled, obviously hearing Kate's snarky comment. "I'll alert the pastry chef to start pumping out annoyingly tiny tartlets."

The line went dead, and I slid the phone down to my lap.

"I take it the industry is already buzzing about Brianna's party?" Kate asked.

"Apparently. I have to give the woman credit, she always seems to land on her feet."

"It's easier when you're landing on piles of cash," Kate said.

She had a point. Brianna did seem to keep herself afloat, not from good press she earned but from PR she bought.

"Hey." Kate nudged me. "Is that who I think it is?"

I followed her line of sight and her outstretched finger. There--

walking along the sidewalk of M Street--was a Santa Claus who appeared to be singing. I rolled down my window and slowed the car. Yep. That was definitely "We Wish You a Merry Christmas" I heard wafting through the air.

I fumbled for my phone. "I should call Reese and tell him we found Kris Kringle Jingle."

"I can't believe he's strolling down the sidewalk like nothing happened." Kate shook her head. "And where did he get a new suit?"

Although we could only see the back of the Santa, we could hear him pretty clearly as he belted out the last few bars of the song. "It's December. Santa costumes can't be too hard to find, although he looks a lot skinnier from the back than I remember."

When Santa took a breath and started singing "Grandma Got Run Over By a Reindeer," Kate and I turned to each other.

"That's not Kris," she said.

I agreed with her, wishing I could get through the traffic and get a good look at the front of this imposter Santa. "Who else would walk around Georgetown singing in a Santa costume?"

"Maybe one of the Salvation Army bell ringers decided to poach the gig now that Kris has disappeared."

"That doesn't seem very Christmassy," I said. "Then again, neither does 'Grandma Got Run Over by a Reindeer.'"

"And it's going to be stuck in my head for the rest of the day," Kate grumbled, grabbing the door handle. "Slow down. I'm getting out."

"What?" We weren't going very fast, but we were moving, and we were in the left lane. I slammed on my brakes as she opened the door. "You're getting out in the middle of the street?"

"I need to give this guy a piece of my mind." She closed the door behind her and scooted through the other cars, waving as they honked at her.

I slid down in my seat, glad once again that I didn't have a Wedding Belles sticker or magnet on my car. Keeping my eyes on Kate as she reached the sidewalk, I drove slowly to catch up with the stopped cars at the light.

She was too far away for me to hear, but I could see Kate walk up to the Santa and wave a finger at him, then stop, gape, and burst into laughter. That was not what I expected. What was even more of a surprise was when Santa turned around and waved at me.

Correction. Fern, dressed from head to toe as Santa Claus, waved at me.

CHAPTER 18

"I'm assuming you have an explanation for why you were wandering around Georgetown singing dodgy Christmas carols," I said to Fern as Kate and I followed him into his salon.

Up close, it was easy to see that Fern's version of Santa was a far cry from Kris Kringle Jingle, or most Santas. His costume had slimming darts at the waist and the wide shiny black belt served to cinch his midsection instead of ring it, with the jacket belling out beneath the belt like a miniskirt. His red velvet pants had a wide white cuff but were not wide-legged and baggy. Somehow, Fern had acquired the only pair of slim-fit Santa pants known to man.

"I beg your pardon." The bells on Fern's costume jingled as he flounced across the highly polished floors and deposited his red sack beside one of the two stylist chairs. "What was wrong with my songs?"

Kate cocked an eyebrow at him. "Grandma Got Run Over by a Reindeer?"

He pulled off his fake beard and deposited it on the ornate wooden credenza in front of the red swivel stylist's chair, his enormous blue topaz ring flashing in the opulent gold mirror on the wall. "A momentary lapse, sweetie. I'd already gone through all the favorites and that little ditty popped into my head."

"I guess a better question is why were you singing carols dressed as Santa in the first place?" I asked, noticing that the usually extravagantly decorated hair salon was even more ornamented than usual, with a frosted Christmas tree glittering at the back and red-and-gold wire ribbon garland draped in swags across the walls with massive bows topping each of the carved gold mirrors. Even the crystal chandeliers were swagged with red ribbon. Along with the usual scent of high-end hair products, the salon smelled faintly of fir tree and cinnamon, and Mariah Carey sang about all she wanted for Christmas faintly in the background.

"For Kris, of course," Fern said, removing his Santa hat and inspecting his hair in the mirror. "His singing is a tradition, and I, for one, don't want to see it lost. These are dark times, girls. We can't lose Santa Claus on top of everything else."

Kate shrugged and exchanged a glance with me. "He's not wrong."

I'd never known how fond of Christmas Fern was or how attached he'd been to Kris Kringle Jingle's carols. "That's a really nice sentiment, but how do you plan to take up Kris's job and do yours? I assume your clients aren't taking the holidays off."

"Sadly, no." Fern sighed, hiking up his shiny black belt as he headed to the mini refrigerator he kept behind a folding, tufted screen covered in red silk. "The holidays are prime time for blowouts and updos for parties, not to mention every floozy in town needs her roots done before New Year's."

Kate touched a hand to her own hair and walked closer to one of the mirrors to look at it. "Don't remind me."

Fern disappeared behind the screen, only his red velvet derrière poking out as he bent over. "Remember, Kate, we aren't coloring your hair, we're merely restoring it back to its original shade."

"Maybe when she was five," I muttered.

Kate ignored me and flopped into one of the red chairs and swiveled it in a circle. "Should I remind Fern how long it's been since you got a haircut?"

I didn't have to look at my long, auburn hair pulled up into a high ponytail to be reminded just how long I'd let it grow. "You know I don't pay attention to my hair when we're busy."

"Which is always," Kate said. "I'm surprised he hasn't thrown a smock around you already."

To be honest, so was I. Fern usually relished any excuse to drag me into his chair and give me a trim, since I never remembered to schedule appointments. Today, he seemed to be too preoccupied by the Santa drama to give my split ends a second thought.

Fern emerged from behind the screen with a bottle of champagne in one hand and three glass flutes in the other. "I'm hoping I can get some substitute Santas to take the shifts I can't."

I eyed the champagne. "I hope this isn't your way of buttering us up, because we really don't have the time--"

"Don't be silly." Fern let out a peal of laughter. "I know you two can't do it, plus I've heard you sing."

I tried not to take too much offense at that, but I was relieved he wasn't going to try to sweet-talk us into donning Santa suits.

"Let me guess," Kate said as she took one of the champagne flutes from Fern. "Is one of your stand-in Santas short with jet-black hair?"

Fern beamed as he handed me a glass. "Did the old girl tell you?"

"I'm a good guesser," Kate said as Fern poured her some bubbly, and the cranberries that had been in the bottom of her flute bobbed to the surface. "Who else loves dressing up as much as you do?"

I gave his outfit the once-over. "I hate to be the one to tell you, but I don't think this suit will fit her. Not unless she wears platform boots."

Fern poured champagne into my glass and giggled. "She's not wearing my suit. I had this custom-made, sweetie. Leatrice has her own Santa suit."

Why was I not surprised about either statement?

"So you and Leatrice are going to pick up the slack from Kris Kringle Jingle and sing carols all the way until Christmas?" Kate asked.

"Only until Kris returns," Fern said, "and I doubt he'll lay low until Christmas. This is his favorite time of the year."

I took a sip of champagne and the bubbles tickled my throat as I swallowed. "You're the second person we've talked to today who seems sure Kris is alive."

"You know me. I'm an optimist." Fern filled his own glass and set the bottle on the nearest credenza.

Kate raised an eyebrow at me. Fern was usually the first person to predict the sky was falling or take to his bed over the new Pantone color of the year being a shade that was horrible for his complexion.

"You were convinced that something awful had happened just yesterday," I reminded him. "What changed your mind?"

Fern's gaze darted around the shop as he drained his glass and reached for the bottle of bubbly. "I decided to get into the Christmas spirit and think positive thoughts."

I narrowed my eyes at him. "What aren't you telling us?"

Fern poured himself another glass, his hands trembling slightly. "Can't a jolly old elf change his mind?" He upended the bottle completely and shook the last few drops into his glass. "Better get us another."

When he'd slipped off the chair and bustled off to the back of the salon, I turned to Kate. "What's gotten into him, do you think?"

"You know this season makes people crazy, and Fern's already got a head start." Kate spun herself around in the chair. "Maybe he can't deal with the idea of Kris being seriously hurt or dead and has decided to be delusional instead of realistic."

That made some sort of twisted sense, although I couldn't help thinking that Fern's about-face was sudden. "You don't think he'd keep something from us, do you?"

"Fern?" Kate laughed, stopping her spinning chair with one foot. "When have you ever known him to be able to keep a secret?"

She had a point. If you wanted the world to know something, you told Fern.

A shriek from the back made us both freeze, exchange a quick look, then run off to find the source of the screaming. We pushed through a heavy brocade curtain dividing the salon from the back storage area and found Fern standing with his hands pressed to his cheeks.

"What's wrong?" I asked.

Fern swung around to face us both, waving a hand at the door that led to the back alleyway standing ajar. "I've been robbed."

CHAPTER 19

My fiancé strode to the door that still hung open, running a hand through his hair. "So this was standing open when you came in?"

Fern nodded, his fingers pressed to his lips. "I only use the back door for the occasional delivery. I don't use it to come in and out."

Kate stood next to him, rubbing his arm while she held a freshly opened bottle of bubbly in her other hand. She'd been refilling both of their glasses since Fern had discovered the break-in and called the police.

Reese hadn't been the first to arrive. His partner, Detective Hobbes, had beaten him there, and a pair of uniformed officers were checking the back alley.

It had been a while since I'd seen my fiancé's partner. Since he'd started a long-distance relationship with our go-to cake baker who lived in Scotland, he'd been using lots of accumulated time off. Despite his frequent overseas trips, not much had changed with the slightly paunchy and slightly frumpy detective. Every time I saw him in his rumpled clothes, I was amazed he was dating our glamorous baker friend. But I'd seen lots of odd pairings in my years planning weddings--nothing should have surprised me anymore. One thing I knew for sure, you couldn't use reason or logic to explain love.

"And you're sure you didn't leave it open?" Hobbes asked, bending down to inspect the lock and smoothing a palm over his light-brown comb-over. "It doesn't look forced."

Kate topped off his glass, and Fern tossed it back. "I've had no reason to open it over the past few days, but I also don't remember checking it."

Reese looked over from where he stood next to Hobbes. "And no one else has a key?"

Fern cleared his throat. "Well, I've given keys to stylists who've worked for me so they can accept deliveries when I'm not here, and I had a receptionist for a hot minute and she still has a key, and I gave the shop owner next door and Leatrice a copy just in case I ever locked myself out."

We all stared at him.

"And then I keep a spare on top of the doorsill."

Reese dragged a hand over his face as he shook his head. "So pretty much anyone could have walked in here?"

Fern held his glass out to Kate, who promptly filled it. "But why would they? I don't have anything to steal except industrial-sized bottles of shampoo."

"And champagne," Kate reminded him, holding up the bottle.

The two uniformed officers walked inside from the back door. I recognized one as the rookie we'd talked to at the station and felt my cheeks warm as I saw a flash of recognition when he spotted Kate and me.

"Nothing outside to tell us who might have done this," he said. If he did remember us, he didn't say anything.

"Thanks," Hobbes said, waving for them both to follow him out front as he glanced at his partner. "We'll leave you to wrap this up."

Reese nodded, thumping the detective on the back. I could tell from the quick look exchanged between the two men that they thought the call had been a waste of time. I was starting to agree with them.

I noticed the rookie cop look at Kate as he passed, blushing when she winked at him. I wanted to thank him for not mentioning that he'd met us before, but I hoped Kate's wink conveyed our gratitude. If

Reese noticed the exchange, he didn't remark on it. Of course, it wasn't unusual for Kate to flirt with cops. Or firemen or paramedics or security guards. Come to think of it, it would have been more unusual if she hadn't.

"So what *is* missing?" Reese asked once the rest of the police had left.

Fern swiveled his head to take in the storage area and the floor-to-ceiling shelving units. Fluffy beige towels were scattered in one corner along with a cellophane-wrapped family-size pack of toilet paper. "Not much. The towels have been strewn all over the floor, but I don't think any are gone. It looks like someone flattened my toilet paper, and I seem to be missing a box of biscotti."

Reese's gaze flicked to me, and I could tell he was battling between frustration and amusement. "So we're not looking for a hardened criminal, just someone who was in the mood for cookies and likes to squeeze the Charmin."

Fern slid his eyes to my detective fiancé. "Are you saying this isn't a crime?"

"Not a violent one, and if the intruder used a key, it was barely a B and E."

Fern blinked at him.

"Breaking and entering," I said in a low voice.

"Thank you, Annabelle." Sarcasm dripped off Fern's voice.

Kate tapped one high-heeled foot on the tile floor. "I would suspect Brianna, but if it was her, I'd have expected her to do more damage."

"Kate's right," I said. "Given her recent track record, Brianna would have broken mirrors or trashed the place. The intruder didn't even appear to leave this storage area. They clearly didn't intend to vandalize or steal."

Reese eyed the towels. "If it was cold out, I'd think it was someone sneaking in to get warm."

Fern's face lit up. "What if it was Kris?"

Now it was my turn to study the towels with interest. "Then where's the blood? His Santa suit was pretty bloody. If he was injured badly enough to bleed like that, wouldn't he be dripping blood?"

We all looked at the clean floor and unblemished towels. Fern's shoulders sagged.

"I don't think we should rule it out," Reese said. "We haven't gotten the results back on the bloody Santa suit yet, and we can't be sure the blood belongs to Kris."

"You think someone else was injured that badly while wearing Kris's Santa suit?" I tried to keep the disbelief from my voice, but it didn't work. It seemed out of character for Kris to let someone else wear his beloved suit and even stranger that person would then get severely wounded in it. "Then why did Kris disappear?"

"And where's the naked, injured person?" Kate asked. "Because whoever was in that suit, ditched it and managed to run off."

"I checked all the hospitals," Reese admitted. "None of them report a patient with injuries consistent with that amount of blood loss in the past few days."

I swallowed hard. That meant that either the person was lying low or they were dead. I turned to Fern. "I think now would be a good time to explain why you're so sure Kris is alive."

Reese walked over to stand next to me, putting a hand casually around my waist. The heat from his body sent a small jolt of pleasure through me, and I almost forgot what I'd asked Fern.

Fern let out a long breath and shrugged. "If you must know, I learned a little more about Kris after you left yesterday."

"From the other homeless people?" Reese asked.

Fern nodded. "Did you know that Kris served in the Navy, and he did two tours in Vietnam?"

"No," I said, leaning back into my fiancé. "I don't know much about him, aside from the fact that he has a nice singing voice and gives great compliments."

"Well, he didn't talk about it much, but he did a bunch of covert ops with naval intelligence over there."

"Wow." Kate shook her head. "I never would have guessed."

"I doubt it's something you advertised much when you came back," I said. "So what does him being in the military have to do with your changing your mind?"

"If Kris survived a war, he's smart enough not to get killed here," Fern said.

Kate took a swig from her champagne flute. "He has a point. If he was involved in covert ops, he must know how to lay low."

I glanced around the storage room. "And how to sneak into a building."

Reese leaned down and whispered in my ear. "I wouldn't call it sneaking if the key is kept over the doorsill."

"You know Kris isn't the only person missing," I reminded Fern.

"At least we know Jeannie is safe," he said.

I'd told Reese soon after he'd arrived, but I'd forgotten to ask him about Kate's claim the cops were watching her. I looked up at him. "Would there be any reason a couple of plainclothes cops would be keeping an eye on her?"

He tilted his head at me. "As far as I know, I'm the only cop who even knows who she is."

He had a point. I turned my attention back to Fern. "There's always the possibility that Stanley might have had something to do with Kris's disappearance."

Reese arched an eyebrow at me. "You think?"

I remembered that I couldn't explain why I thought that or that I'd gotten the inside scoop from one of his fellow cops. "He did find the suit. Maybe that was because he was dumping it."

Fern gasped. "What an awful thought. You think he's missing because he's a killer on the run? I don't want *him* coming in my salon and squeezing my Charmin."

"We don't know for sure," I said, quickly, avoiding my fiancé's piercing gaze. "It's just a theory."

"Which you promised not to come up with," Kate said out of the corner of her mouth.

"It came to me on the fly," I said, more for Reese's benefit.

Reese laughed. "I'm surprised you only have one theory at this point."

I didn't know whether to be offended or flattered.

Fern closed the back door and straightened his white fur collar. "Be that as it may, I'd better get back to caroling. Leatrice isn't starting her shift for another hour."

"Do I want to know?" Reese asked me, his low voice tickling my neck.

"Probably not," I told him, glad that he'd taken my murder theory in stride. "Just don't be surprised if you see a really short Santa around Georgetown."

I felt Reese's phone buzz in his jeans pocket and he retrieved it, looking quickly at the screen before answering. "Mike Reese here."

I watched as his face became solemn and then grim. He thanked the person on the other end and hung up, sliding the phone back into his jeans.

"Bad news?" I asked.

"I'm not sure. One floater they pulled out of the river, which is never fun. And a beat cop just found a guy knocked out cold and hog-tied down near the harbor with enough meth on him to kill an elephant."

"How could that be good news?" Kate asked.

Reese rubbed a hand down his scruffy cheeks. "The guy who was tied up runs a seedy strip club. We've suspected him of using the club as a front for drug trafficking for years, but have never been able to get anything to stick."

"Why do you look so conflicted?" I asked, knowing my fiancé's expression.

"Not so much conflicted as perplexed," he said. "The guy was wearing a Santa suit when they found him."

CHAPTER 20

I checked my phone again before dropping it onto the couch next to me. No text from Reese, although I didn't really expect one. I knew he was busy processing a murder scene, and I cringed as I thought about the body pulled from the river. Then I thought about the man found in a Santa suit, and wondered about all the criminals turning up decked out in suits or hats. First Kris Kringle Jingle goes missing, then his suit is found and the guy who found it goes missing, then criminals start turning up wearing Santa garb. Either someone had a thing against Santa or a weird Santa fetish. Reese had made us all promise not to read too much into it, making me swear I wouldn't take this as a reason to get more involved in the case.

"You don't have to tell me twice," Kate had told him as he'd left for the waterfront and the dead body they'd pulled out. "I've had enough of floaters, thank you very much."

Fern had agreed with her, looking a bit green as we'd walked him out to one of his stylist chairs.

I wanted to remind them the one body we'd found floating in a pond could hardly have been considered a floater since she'd barely been in the water for half an hour before we'd spotted her, but I thought it best not to remind my fiancé about the latest murder investigation we'd meddled in. Like Kate and Fern, I'd promised Reese to leave this case to the DC police and had given him a quick kiss as he'd dashed out the door. And I'd meant it. Of course, that was before I had so much time to mull things over.

Sinking back into my couch, I let out a deep sigh, soaking up the quiet. For the first time in days, there was no one in my apartment but me, and the silence was blissful. As bad as I felt about my fiancé being called to a murder scene, I was grateful for the rare moments of solitude. I didn't even have an urge to think about why Kris was still missing.

It wasn't that I didn't love living with Reese. I did. But after living by myself for so many years, I was still adjusting to having someone around who never left. My evenings watching trashy TV while I caught up on paperwork had fallen by the wayside, and I never ate cupcakes for dinner anymore.

Propping my bare feet up on the coffee table, I glanced at the alphabetized rehearsal dinner place cards stacked next to the ceremony programs all folded and tied with ivory ribbon. Not only did I finally have the place to myself, Kate had helped me knock out most of the weekend's wedding prep before she'd dashed off to meet her mystery man for dinner. The panic that had been fluttering in my stomach all week had lessened somewhat after we'd finished some of the tedious work that always took hours the week of a wedding.

We'd both learned our lessons years ago and would never dream about leaving place card alphabetizing and program tying until the last minute. It was bad enough when clients gave us changes to the seating the day of the wedding, but after being burned by one too many procrastinating brides and being forced to stay up until the wee hours the night before the wedding, we now insisted on their seating plans a full week before the wedding day. It made my heart sing to see the neat stacks of paper products all ready to go for the weekend.

"One down," I said to myself, knowing we still had plenty to do to plan the New Year's Eve wedding and pull together my engagement/Wedding Belles holiday party.

A quick peek out the darkened windows told me it was later than

I'd realized, and my growling stomach reminded me that I'd survived the day on snacks and champagne. I didn't bother checking the fridge as I contemplated what type of takeout I should order and pulled my phone out of my pocket.

Would Reese be back in time to join me? My mind wandered to the drug dealer dressed up as Santa. Was it possible the man was connected to Kris?

I knew I was under strict orders not to get involved in the case, but I couldn't help wondering why someone would put the low life in a Santa suit and dump him for the police to find. I seriously doubted the strip club owner happened to be dressed as Santa before he was tied up, but what if he was? Was someone out to get Santas in DC? I thought about what Fern had told us. Kris had been involved in covert ops in Vietnam. Was it possible that Kris wasn't a victim? Could he be some sort of Santa vigilante? But what about Stanley? No one saw him actually find the bloody suit. What if he had been trying to ditch it when the cop appeared, and he'd had to pretend he'd found it? He might have knocked off Kris—either accidentally or in the heat of the moment—and gone on the run out of fear and guilt.

Shaking my head, I stood up. No way. I much preferred to think Kris had snuck into Fern's storage room than a killer was on the loose.

As I put the neatly stacked place cards and programs back in their boxes, I heard a sharp rap on the door. So much for my peaceful evening. I resigned myself to the high probability of it being Leatrice fully dressed in a Santa suit and eager to pump me for information on the murder she'd no doubt heard about over her police scanner. I opened the door and blinked a few times.

"Richard," I said as he pushed past me into the apartment. "Did we have plans?"

"Not per se." He dropped his man bag on the couch and set a paper bag with handles on the floor. Hermès spilled out of the leather bag and began scampering from one end of the couch to the other, sniffing vigorously.

"Do I smell food?" I inhaled the savory aroma that seemed to be emanating from the paper bag.

"I'm assuming you haven't eaten yet, am I right?" Richard

answered my question with one of his own, his eyes flitting to my boxes of paper products on the coffee table.

"You assume correctly. Kate and I were knocking out some of the work for the wedding, and you know my rule about food and drink near paper products."

Richard picked up the paper bag and headed for the kitchen, giving me a quick look over his shoulder. "You mean the rule I taught you? Yes, I'm familiar with it, darling."

"Right." It was hard to remember all the things Richard had taught me over the years, since he'd taken me under his wing from almost the moment I'd moved to DC and opened Wedding Belles, sharing all his tips and tricks for surviving the world of events.

His dark choppy hair appeared over the divider between the kitchen and living room. "Fern told me that our detective was called out to a murder. I knew that meant you'd be left to your own devices for dinner, and we all know what that means."

Our detective? I wondered when *my* fiancé had become our detective, but I decided not to say anything. The bromance Richard had going on with Reese was better than the thinly veiled hostility he used to have for the man he'd once considered his usurper.

"You know I'm fully capable of feeding myself," I said, perching on the back of my couch and petting Hermès absently on the head as he settled into a spot.

Richard snorted from the kitchen. "I've seen your refrigerator, Annabelle, and it's barely changed since you started cohabitating."

"We both work a lot," I said, in my own defense.

"You know I'm not one for gender stereotypes," he said, coming out of the kitchen wearing a pink toile apron and carrying two pasta bowls. "But one of you two is going to have to learn how to cook. I thought it might be the detective, but I didn't take into account his erratic schedule and how often you'd be solo."

I followed him to the dining table, breathing in the rich scent as he set down the bowls. "Maybe you can be our live-in cook?"

He arched a perfectly coifed brow at me. "Not with the way you keep house."

"And we might not have room for PJ, as well," I said, referencing the significant other we'd met for the first time at Leatrice's wedding.

Richard's cheeks colored, and he hurried back to the kitchen. "If three's a crowd, four would be a disaster."

"You are bringing him to the party on Sunday, aren't you?" I asked as I sat down in front of one of the steaming bowls of pasta.

Richard returned with a tiny ceramic dish he placed on the floor, and Hermès immediately leapt from the couch and rushed over, while Richard bustled back to the kitchen, skillfully dodging the eager dog and my question.

I leaned over and peered at the contents of the dish. "Your dog eats pancetta?"

"He has very discerning taste," Richard said as he emerged from the kitchen again, this time with two wine glasses and an opened bottle. "Tell me if the nutmeg is too much in the carbonara. Nigella swears by it, but she is British."

I decided not to call Richard out on changing the subject, as I swirled my fork in the lightly sauced spaghetti. I suspected he was keeping his personal life close to his chest because he didn't want PJ getting a sense of how crazy our crew was and running for the hills. Not a bad plan. I'd been lucky Reese had a high tolerance for crazy.

"I didn't know you and Fern talked often," I said. "What else did he tell you?"

Richard shrugged as he filled my glass halfway with white wine. "Just that he'd had a break-in, and Reese had been called away early because they'd found a body."

"Did he tell you about the other guy they found?" I took a bite and savored the rich flavor of the crunchy pancetta.

"Some lowlife club owner tied up like he'd gotten on the wrong side of a dominatrix." Richard wrinkled his nose. "Fern's words, not mine."

"He was found wearing a Santa suit."

Richard's fork froze halfway to his mouth. "That explains it."

"Explains what?"

"Why Fern called me and was so insistent I come over here and keep an eye on you. He kept saying it was his fault that you were going to be sucked back in like Michael Corleone in *The Godfather III.*"

I swallowed a too-hot mouthful and washed it down with a cold gulp of wine. "He compared me to the Godfather?"

"I thought it was a bit much considering our latest run-in with the mob, but now I get it." He eyed me. "Frankly, I'm surprised you're sitting here so calmly."

I rolled my eyes. "I promised Reese I wouldn't meddle."

"And you were serious about that?"

"Of course," I said, twirling spaghetti around my fork. "I've turned over a new leaf. Besides, Reese is still looking for Kris, so I know it's in good hands. And if there's a connection with all the other Santa crimes, he'll find it."

As if on cue, the door opened and my fiancé stumbled inside, his clothes disheveled and dirty.

Richard's mouth dropped open. "You didn't personally drag the body out of the Potomac, did you?"

Reese didn't even register surprise at seeing Richard in our apartment as he collapsed onto the couch, and Hermès scampered over and began licking his hand.

Richard sucked in a sharp breath. "Hermès! You do not know where that's been."

"You were saying something about his discerning taste?" I said, earning myself a pointed look as I got up to join Reese on the couch.

"You look like you need some pasta," Richard headed for the kitchen, wagging a finger at the little Yorkie who followed him. "And now *you* need a good teeth brushing, young man."

"How did things go with the body?" I asked, sitting next to Reese and brushing a loose strand of dark hair off his face.

"Well, it wasn't an accident." Reese rubbed a hand across his forehead. "The guy was strangled before he was tossed into the river."

My stomach turned. "What about the drug dealing Santa?"

He shook his head. "It's not my case."

"But shouldn't you be involved since it might be connected to the other Santa cases?"

Reese sighed. "The way things are going, I won't sleep if I take on all the cases with a Santa element to them."

"But what if the Santa crimes are connected?" When he didn't answer, I shook my head. "Someone needs to be working that angle."

Richard let out a tortured breath behind us. "Why do I feel like I know who that someone will be?"

CHAPTER 21

"He has a point, you know," Kate said as we walked along M Street the next day.

I'd insisted we spend the morning wrapping up the details for Saturday as well as calling potential vendors for our New Year's Eve wedding, then Kate had convinced me that we needed a break to stretch our legs and do some holiday shopping. As usual, I'd been too caught up in work to find presents for anyone, and, as of that morning, Kate had added a Secret Santa present to my long list.

"Who has a point?" I asked, glancing at a brightly decorated store window flocked with white paint to make it look like snow. Ironic, since I was almost sweating in the spring-like weather, even though I only wore a white button-down and jeans.

"Richard, of course. If Reese isn't working all the Santa cases, aren't you going to be tempted to connect them yourself? I know it's already killing you that Stanley is missing and we don't know why."

I shook my head as I dodged a group of giggling college students attempting to take a selfie while they walked down the sidewalk. "I do have some self-control, you know."

"Mmmhmm." She sounded far from convinced. "Have they given up looking for Kris?"

I shrugged. "Reese hasn't, but I think only as a favor to our friends.

They haven't made much headway with that, although I want to side with Fern. He's not dead even though he hasn't turned up."

"But another guy in a Santa suit has turned up. And some in Santa hats."

"Yep," I said. "I guess it could be a coincidence, but that seems unlikely."

"But what's the connection, aside from both being Santa? A homeless vet and a dodgy club owner don't seem like a likely pairing. And then a couple of thieves?"

"Your guess is as good as mine," I said. "Maybe this club owner was involved in whatever Kris saw that made him freak out enough to go into hiding. Kris could be hiding to avoid falling victim to the same fate. Maybe someone is picking off Santas one by one."

"And you think that someone is Stanley?"

"Well, I hadn't before, but now I do."

She spun on me. "See? I knew you'd been thinking about it."

"Thinking about it? Sure. But I don't have the time to do anything about it. Our to-do list is a mile long. When would I fit in a murder investigation?"

Kate gave me a sidelong glance. "You're very resourceful, Annabelle. And sneakier than you look."

"Thanks, I think."

"We did get a lot done today," she admitted. "Once our New Year's Eve bride signs the contracts we requested, it's only a matter of confirming details."

"We got lucky she was so burned out from working with Brianna that she gave us carte blanche in picking vendors."

Kate held up one palm. "Do *not* say that name again. I still haven't come up with the proper retribution for that tire slasher."

I wanted to tell her that we weren't 100 percent positive Brianna had been the one to pop her tires, but not even I believed that. "Maybe we should put the brakes on this feud. I think we've come out on the losing end, so far."

"So far," Kate said, her eyes narrowed.

I sighed. I guess we weren't going to take the high road, so I decided to change the subject. "I have no idea what to get for Secret

Santa this year. It's so hard to find something that anyone from our group would like, and now we're going to have a bunch of cops in the mix."

Kate paused in front of The Paper Source, tapping her chin. "I forgot about the extra guests for the engagement party. Maybe we should do the Secret Santa just for our crew after the party."

"That's a good idea," I said, glancing at the large paper nutcrackers and ballerinas perched atop shiny, gold boxes in the store window. "I'd hate to invite Reese's friends to an engagement party and ask them to bring a Secret Santa gift, too. That seems like a lot."

"Agreed." Kate held open the tall glass doors framed in pink. "I don't know how you're going to top the Llamanoes you gave last year."

We walked into the store, the usual tables of gifts piled high with holiday-themed offerings--a stack of mistletoe tea towels next to a red, felt pom-pom Christmas stocking, and an entire table devoted to colorful advent calendars, some of them three-dimensional and one of them featuring "Twelve Days of Christmas" socks. Instrumental holiday music played overhead, and the store smelled like paper and cinnamon air freshener.

Kate stopped at the end of the ramp leading into the shop. "I may have found something to beat the Llamanoes." She held up a box featuring a June Cleaver look-alike. "An inflatable turkey."

"What if Richard ended up with that?" I asked.

She frowned. "Good point. He might not be amused. He's never appreciated food humor." Her expression brightened. "But here's a set of tea towels of dogs dressed in pajamas."

"He might like that *too* much."

Kate grinned at me. "Another good point. We probably shouldn't encourage the dressing the dog like a human thing."

I picked up an inflatable set of antlers with rings to toss over them, labeled "Reindeer Games." "I'd say this might be fun if I didn't think Leatrice would want to wear them twenty-four seven."

"Then it's down to the Screaming Goat." Kate held up a box that contained a plastic goat standing on a plastic stump, pressing a button that made the thing let out a high-pitched scream.

I gave her a look.

"What?" She pressed the button again. "I feel like this goat every time Meltdown Maddie calls."

One of our spring brides had a tendency to overreact about everything and often ended up hyperventilating over the phone while we listened to her hunt for a paper bag. "Maybe we should go with something less hysterical."

Kate looked at the goat. "You're right. It sounds too much like Richard when his waiters fold the napkins wrong."

I caught a glimpse of a pair of fully dressed Santa Clauses walking past the store, but quickly realized it wasn't Kris and felt a pang of sadness. The Salvation Army Santas still worked in Georgetown, and it was most likely a couple of them. I remembered what Jeannie had said about the jealous Santas, and a shiver went through me. I hated thinking of every chubby man in a red suit as a potential murderer. It really put a damper on my Christmas cheer.

"I think I need some caffeine and sugar before I can handle any more cheesy holiday gift ideas," I said, feeling my sadness shift into shopping malaise.

"Cheesy?" Kate pretended to be affronted as she held up a set of elf drink markers with the beefy plastic elves wearing nothing but red-and-green hot pants and suspenders.

I laughed. "I feel like you own that outfit."

She cocked an eyebrow at me. "You might be right." She put down the sexy elves and linked her arm through mine. "It's not too early for a cupcake, is it?"

"I don't think it's ever too early for a cupcake, since they're just muffins with a fancy topping."

We headed out of the store, and I was grateful to be walking again. Shopping had never been my thing, which was one reason I bought most of my clothes online, to Richard's eternal horror. We turned down Thomas Jefferson Street, the road sloping down toward the canal and further on to the Potomac River and the harbor. I spotted the pink bicycle tied up outside our favorite bakery with flowers brimming from its basket, and I quickened my step. Baked & Wired cupcakes always improved my mood.

After crossing the bridge over the canal and seeing one of the old-fashioned canal boats tied to the shore, we ducked inside the glass-fronted bakery. I breathed in the heady aroma of coffee and icing, my gaze instantly drawn to the long counter covered in cupcakes, cookies, and cakes topped with glass domes. One tall shelving unit held holiday gift sets along with cellophane bags of peanut brittle and their trademark Hippie Crack granola tied with festive red ribbon.

"I'll grab coffees," Kate said, pointing to the coffee bar on the other side of the store. "Can you get me a uniporn cupcake?"

"Uniporn?" I repeated.

She winked at me. "The full name is 'uniporn and rainho', but they'll know what you mean."

This would be fun to order, I thought as Kate walked away, and I proceeded to the bakery counter. After inspecting the day's offerings, I ordered Kate's uniporn--which appeared to be funfetti with pink icing--along with a razmanian devil, dirty chai, chocolate doom, red velvet, and coconut.

"Hungry?" Kate asked as I met her at the door with a box of half a dozen cupcakes.

I took the paper cup of coffee she held out to me. "These aren't all for us. I thought Buster and Mack might need some cheering up. The holidays are always crazy for them, and Kris is still missing, which I know worries them."

"Good idea." She squeezed my arm. "Cupcakes always make me feel better."

We stepped outside, and I rested the box and my coffee on one of the empty French wire tables. Opening the box, I handed Kate her pink cupcake with heart sprinkles on the top and plucked out the razmanian devil with white frosting and single sugar heart perched on top.

Kate tapped her cupcake's wax paper wrapper against mine. "Cheers."

I took a bite of my cupcake, savoring the burst of flavor as I bit through the thick lemon buttercream and reached the raspberry jam center. She was right. Even though I'd gotten no shopping done, Kris Kringle Jingle was still missing, and now one of his friends was dead, the rush of sugar made me feel better. At least we had the New Year's Eve wedding well in hand and hadn't sustained any further property damage. If the temperature would dip below seventy degrees, I might consider the day a success.

Looking over Kate's head, I saw another Santa crossing the street at the intersection with M. Now that Santas were missing and Santa crimes on the rise—and in my mind, they were also suspects in Kris's disappearance—I seemed to see them everywhere. I felt a small surge of hope as I squinted at the red-suited figure a block away. Even from the distance, I could tell it wasn't Kris, and my heart sank. Santa glanced our way, then jerked back around, quickened his pace to a near run, and disappeared down M Street.

"Did you see that?" I asked Kate, but she was too involved in her cupcake to have noticed. Was I imagining things or had this Santa been wearing hipster glasses?

"What?" Kate mumbled through a mouthful.

"Nothing." I dismissed the feeling that Santa had been spooked by something, glancing around me and seeing nothing but a few tourists. Tucking my partially eaten cupcake back into the box, I closed it again, balancing the cupcake box and my coffee as we crossed the street toward Lush. The bell jingled overhead as we pushed through the front door, but instead of cheery Christmas carols, we were met with the sound of shrieking.

"That's no screaming goat," Kate said, wiping a dab of icing off her mouth. "And it doesn't sound like baby Merry, either."

We followed the sounds to the back of the shop where Buster sat with his head in his hands and Mack paced behind him, his hands in the air as he wailed. When he saw us, he stopped.

"You got my message?"

Kate looked at me. "What message?"

"We just called your office," Buster said. "We were about to call your cells."

"What's going on?" I asked, feeling a nervous flutter in my chest.

Mack began pacing again. "The flower order for this weekend's wedding? It's gone."

I stared at him. "Our wedding at the Four Seasons?"

Buster nodded, mutely.

"What do you mean, gone?" Kate said.

"When our guys went to the wholesaler this morning to pick it up, they said one of our other guys had picked it up already," Buster said. "As soon as they opened."

"We don't have other guys," Mack said, throwing his hands in the air again. "Someone stole our flowers and there's no time to get more, even if the entire city wasn't sold out."

Kate turned to me. "We're going to need more cupcakes."

CHAPTER 22

"I don't understand," Kate said, pacing next to Mack. "How can someone just waltz in and take an entire flower order?"

"The person apparently had our vendor number and knew enough to be convincing," Buster told her. He now stood at the cappuccino machine, a red velvet cupcake in one hand and the machine's metal coffee basket in the other. "And had a U-Haul van."

"So it had to be someone who had insider information into your business." I took a sip of the hot mocha Kate had gotten me, as I perched on one of the metal barstools around the long, high table. "Did the people at the warehouse recognize whomever picked up the flowers?"

"They were wearing a Santa suit," Mack said.

"What?" I nearly slipped off the stool.

Kate threw her hands up. "This is ridiculous. Are we the only people *not* wearing Santa suits?"

"Why?" Buster asked. "Who else is wearing them?"

"Aside from Fern and Leatrice as they try to fill in for Kris, only every criminal who's getting caught recently," I told them, giving them a brief rundown of all the Santa-related busts.

"That's pretty odd," Mack admitted, "but I doubt a criminal would have any use for our flowers."

"True." I settled myself back on the stool. "So we're back to someone who knows your business. Do you have any disgruntled employees who've left recently?"

Mack gave me a scandalized look. "Disgruntled? I would hope not. We take good care of our staff."

Buster fired up the milk frothing wand, which screeched for a moment before he turned it off again. "But we do have freelance staff that works for other florists. Maybe all this was a big misunderstanding and one of our freelancers got confused."

Leave it to my Christian biker friends to always look for the best in people. I wished he was right, but my gut told me his hope was misplaced.

"Then why haven't you gotten a call?" Kate asked, spinning on her heel and walking a brisk path across the width of the room. "By this point, whichever florist got the order should know it isn't theirs, right?"

Buster nodded reluctantly. "Right. We had an unusually large amount of birch branches and white hydrangea. It wasn't your typical Christmastime order."

Since we were trying to recreate a winter wonderland inside the Four Seasons hotel, everything about the decor was white. This wasn't a case where we could substitute a bunch of potted poinsettias and call it a day.

Mack paused his pacing for a moment as Buster thrust a cappuccino at him. "Where are we going to find that much large head white hydrangea by Saturday?"

"I would suggest we creep into people's gardens," Kate said, "but December isn't the season for it."

"And the wholesaler doesn't have any more or can't rush any more to you?" I asked, eyeing the open box of cupcakes in front of me. I'd finished my razmanian devil, but the stress of the situation had the coconut calling my name.

Buster returned to the table, cradling an oversized round coffee cup. "Not by Saturday. Most of the product we ordered was Dutch, so there isn't time for it to fly over and clear customs. I called around for anything local, but there's nothing."

I tore my gaze from the cupcakes and took a deep breath, inhaling the rich aroma of Buster's freshly brewed cappuccinos. "What are our options? Change the look?"

Kate shook her head. "The bride will freak."

"Agreed," I said. "Two days before the wedding is not the time to spring this on a bride. I know none of us want to use silk."

Mack sucked in a breath so sharply I looked around to see if Richard had walked in. "Lush does not use fake flowers."

I held up my hands. "It was just a last-resort suggestion. Silks have come a long way, you know."

"Even if we bought out every craft store in the area, I doubt we'd have enough white hydrangea," Buster said.

I took a gulp of coffee and sat up straighter. "Then we need to find your flowers. Someone clearly has them. Someone who has a grudge against you."

"Or against us," Kate said, slapping her hand on the metal table and making me jump. "This has Brianna written all over it."

Before I could tell her that was a ridiculous thought, I paused to really consider it. Brianna did know we used Lush almost exclusively. She also knew we had a wedding at the Four Seasons on Saturday, plus it wasn't out of the realm of possibility that she could have hired one of Buster and Mack's freelancers. The guy might not have even known he was doing something sneaky if she'd told him it was for her wedding. Brianna's smarmy Southern accent seemed to work like a charm on most men. And I wouldn't put it past our rival to try to sabotage us so dramatically. If she was resorting to vandalism, she was already pretty unhinged.

"You might be right," I said.

Mack's mouth gaped. "You think another wedding planner is behind this?"

Buster adjusted the motorcycle goggles perched on his bald head. "I know she's never used us before, but this seems extreme."

"It's not about you," Kate said. "It's about us. She's livid because her New Year's Eve bride fired her and hired us last week. She refused to turn the venue contract she'd signed over to the bride, and is holding her own party there instead on New Year's Eve just so we'd have to scramble for a last-minute venue. We're also pretty sure she's the one who slashed all four of my tires outside Annabelle's apartment."

Buster's mug clattered to the table. "She slashed your tires?"

"It sounds like we need to add her to our prayer list." Mack shook his head, his expression solemn. "All that hate in her heart must be a burden."

"You need to pray that I don't kill her," Kate muttered.

"If Brianna did take the flowers, where would she put them?" I asked.

Kate drummed her manicured fingers on the table. "Didn't she open that office space down near the intersection of M and Key Bridge?"

"You're right," I said. "It's upstairs over a bicycle shop or something. I'm sure the rent still costs her father a fortune since it's in Georgetown. It wouldn't look suspicious for a business to get a large flower delivery in Georgetown, but it would raise eyebrows if she had a truck full of flowers delivered to her apartment, wherever that is."

"Capitol Hill," Kate said. "She has a townhouse in Capitol Hill." When she noticed us all staring at her, she added, "Her assistant comes to our wedding assistant happy hours, remember? She told us in the group text that she used to go to Brianna's place on Capitol Hill before they got an office space."

I was both impressed and baffled by the wedding planners who rented expensive office space when so much of our job entailed meetings at venues or other vendors' studios. I knew in Brianna's case, it was more about the status of having a swanky Georgetown address for her business than any real need.

Pulling my phone out of my pocket, I glanced at the time. It was already midafternoon. "Does she go there every day?"

Kate shrugged. "If she does, I doubt she stays late, especially now that she doesn't have any weddings coming up to plan. She's always posting about having dinner at the newest, trendy restaurant, anyway."

"You follow her on social media?" I asked.

She grinned at me. "Only under my Instagram alias, Natasha Moosensquirrel."

Buster nearly spit out a mouthful of coffee, coughing loudly as he attempted to swallow.

"I like to follow some people without having them know it's me," she explained. "And Natasha is my alias when I use my Russian accent at bars to scare off men I'm not interested in."

"And that works?" Mack asked, taking a seat next to Buster.

"Da, darling," she said in a thick accent that brought to mind Rocky and Bullwinkle's cartoon nemesis. "It works like a charm."

I gave my head a shake. "Okay. So we know she probably won't be at her office space after hours. That's when we should go look for the flowers."

"Look for the flowers?" Mack looked from me to Kate as he nervously stroked his goatee. "Do you mean break into her office?"

I grabbed the coconut cupcake and took a bite, closing my eyes to savor it before opening them again and nodding. "If we have to. It isn't stealing if they don't belong to her in the first place."

Buster tilted his head at me. "I guess you're right."

"You don't have to be involved," I said, realizing that not only would it create a crisis of conscience for them, but that we wouldn't exactly be stealthy if we brought the two enormous bikers. Kate and I might be able to pass unnoticed in the back alleys of Georgetown. Buster and Mack were never unnoticed.

"Are you sure?" Mack asked, although I could see he was relieved by the idea of not being involved in a potential crime.

Buster frowned. "Won't you need a way to transport the flowers if you find them?"

"If we find them, we'll call you, and you can bring your van," Kate said. "That way you're only involved in the recovery part of the mission."

Mack put his hands to his cheeks. "What is your fiancé going to say about all this?"

I hadn't thought about Reese. He wasn't going to like this one bit. *If* he found out. "Let's hope he's so pleased I'm not meddling in a criminal investigation that he doesn't notice the rest. He is working late tonight, so hopefully we'll be back before he even notices I'm gone."

"Another foolproof plan," Kate said in her Russian accent. "You'd better be getting him a really good Christmas present, comrade."

CHAPTER 23

"I know I wanted to get back at Brianna," Kate said as she stood in my living room wearing head-to-toe black that looked like it had been painted on. "But I'm not sure if I want to go to jail for it."

"We aren't going to jail." I glanced outside my windows as I pawed through my wedding emergency kit. It was already dark, although I knew Georgetown would be bustling until late into the night. My stomach roiled from nerves, and I regretted that two cupcakes were the bulk of what I'd eaten during the day. Richard was right. I really needed to eat better.

"I can't believe my mini flashlight got swiped."

Kate didn't look surprised. "You know bridesmaids."

It was true that bridesmaids were known for pillaging our wedding supplies, but I couldn't imagine why one had needed a flashlight. Safety pins, hairspray, breath mints, sure. But, a flashlight?

"I guess we'll have to rely on our phones," I said, snapping my boxy metal case shut after retrieving a few bobby pins.

Kate tugged a black knit cap over her hair. "Should I ask what the bobby pins are for?"

"Picking locks," I said as I jammed them into the pocket of my black jeans.

"You can do that?"

I couldn't. "Technically, no, but I figure we should have them just in case."

"In case one of us needs to put our hair up into an emergency French twist?"

I made a face at her. "It can't be that hard. We've learned a lot of things on the fly before. Tying bow ties, folding pocket squares, making a bird of paradise out of a napkin."

"Call me crazy, but I don't want to be covertly watching a how-to YouTube video as we're crouched in front of a door trying to pick the lock."

The first time we'd had to tie actual bow ties for a bridal party, Kate and I had taken turns watching a tutorial on her phone behind one of the enormous pillars in the National Cathedral as we dashed back and forth to the getting-ready room, attempting to make the ties look even. I knew it was a feeling neither one of us ever wanted to repeat, although we'd become experts in tying bow ties since that harrowing day years ago.

"I doubt we'll need to pick a lock," I said. "Doors in Georgetown are notoriously old and rickety."

"So we're going to kick it in? That does not make me feel any better."

I pulled my own hair up into a high ponytail. "I don't know what we're going to do. All I know is that we need those flowers, and if Brianna has them, we're getting them back."

Kate made a fist and punched it into her other hand. "Yeah, we are. But let's go before your fiancé comes home and busts us."

"Good idea." I grabbed my car keys out of my purse, deciding to leave it and any other identification at home. I was looking at the keys, wondering if we should just walk instead of drive, when there was a knock on the door.

"Who do you think it is?" Kate whispered.

"It can't be Reese. He has a key."

"We all have keys," Kate said, reminding me again I should probably change my locks.

"Maybe it's Fern?" I had a good feeling it wasn't Richard, since he'd mentioned giving Hermès a bath when we'd talked earlier. I knew the little dog's bathing ritual included a hot oil treatment and a blowout, so Richard's evening was booked solid.

"Yoo hoo," the voice called through the door.

"Leatrice," Kate and I said at the same time.

Kate motioned to the door. "If you don't open it, she'll just use the key you gave her."

"I didn't give her a key," I reminded her. "She made one using her spy key mold."

Kate rolled her eyes. "You know I don't know any of my neighbors on a first-name basis. You should try it."

"I think that ship has sailed," I said as I opened the door.

Leatrice clapped her hands when she saw us. "Oh, good. You're both here. I need you to give me your honest opinion on my caroling costume."

Her green velvet hoop skirt swung from side to side as she entered my apartment, causing us to move out of the way. The matching cape was lined in white fur, as was the ruffled velvet cap that flopped around her face, and her hands were buried inside a white fur muff.

"It's very..." I began.

"Green," Kate said.

"Too green?" Leatrice asked. "My honeybun is wearing a red velvet suit and a red ribbon around his top hat, and I was going to put Hermès in green and red."

"Hermès is going caroling?" I asked.

Leatrice bobbed her head up and down, and her cap sunk lower on her forehead. "He loves Christmas carols. I haven't run it by Richard yet, but I'm sure he'll agree once he sees the tiny top hat I found."

"As long as you make sure I'm there when you ask him," Kate said.

Leatrice looked us up and down, taking in our attire for the first time since walking inside. "Where are you two off to dressed like Johnny Cash?"

Kate looked down at her outfit and mouthed, *Johnny Cash?*

"Just a work thing," I lied.

My neighbor narrowed her eyes at me. "Kate would never wear this much clothing for a work event."

She had a point. Even though Kate's black pants and scoop neck long-sleeved bodysuit were tight, they did cover her from ankle to wrist. With the black knit cap covering her blond hair, she looked every bit the cat burglar. Emphasis on cat.

Leatrice rubbed her hands together. "You're doing something covert, aren't you?"

"No," I said, at the same time Kate nodded her head.

"I knew it." Leatrice bounced up and down on her toes, making her hoop skirt swing back and forth. "Is it a stakeout? You know I'm excellent at stakeouts."

"It's not a stakeout," I told her. The last time we'd staged an unofficial and probably illegal stakeout, it had ended in my car getting torched and the wrong person being arrested.

"We're trying to find some stolen flowers," Kate said, shrugging when I shot her a look. "What? She would have dragged it out of us, anyway. I'm just saving us all a few tedious steps."

"Stolen flowers?" Leatrice rubbed her chin. "Do you have an idea where they are?"

"We have a guess," I admitted. "But we aren't certain, so we're going to scout it out."

"Understood." Leatrice spun around and headed for the door. "Give me five minutes, and I'll be ready to go."

"Wait," I said, waving my hands. "You can't go with us."

"Why not?" she asked. "I have all the spy and surveillance gear you could ever need, plus I can be your wheelman."

"We don't have a wheelman," Kate said.

"We don't *need* a wheelman," I insisted.

"What if we can't find parking or have to park blocks away?" Kate asked. "This is Georgetown, after all."

"See?" Leatrice beamed before turning and hurrying out the door and down the stairs, holding up her voluminous skirt as it filled up the width of the staircase. "You need me."

I sighed, shooting Kate a look. "What I need is to have my head examined."

"You plan weddings for a living, Annabelle," Kate said. "That's a given."

CHAPTER 24

"Why are we turning here?" I asked Leatrice, clutching the passenger side door handle as she took a wide turn in her ancient Ford Fairmont, the back of the long car seeming to swing around a few seconds after the front.

"To pick up Fern, of course," Leatrice said, adjusting her black fedora and craning her neck around as Kate slid from one end of the back seat to the other. "You okay back there, dear?"

Kate gave a thumbs-up as she righted herself, leaning her head between the driver's and passenger's front seats. "Glad I skipped dinner."

Leatrice glanced over, her face lighting up. "Should we stop for a bite to eat first?"

"We're on a mission to steal back an entire floral order," I said, trying to keep my impatience in check as I eyed the petite woman in a trench coat. "We're not going to the theatre. And tell me why we're picking up Fern."

"He's an excellent lookout." Leatrice didn't slow the car as we bumped up and down over the cobblestoned street and occasionally ran up onto the old trolley rails. "Don't you remember what a help he was when we staked out that murder suspect?"

"I remember him napping," I said.

Leatrice ignored me, pointing ahead of her to a figure all in black standing on the sidewalk. "There he is."

Fern waited outside his salon, although the lights inside the narrow, glass-fronted shop were out and it looked locked up tight. I blinked a few times as we slowed down next to him.

"Did you tell him to dress like a cat?" Kate asked.

Leatrice stopped the car, waving at him through the window. "I told him we were going to be cat burglars."

"That explains the dominatrix outfit," I said as Fern hopped in the back seat in his skintight black catsuit complete with Catwoman face mask with small pointy ears.

"Nice suit." Kate nodded appreciatively. "I might have to borrow it from you someday."

"It's a perfect size eight." Fern smoothed one hand over the shiny fabric. "Just like me."

I twisted around to face the back seat as Leatrice pulled away from the curb. "Just to be clear, we are going to Brianna's office to look for the flower order that was stolen from the wholesaler this morning. It's crucial that no one sees us and even more crucial that no one tells my fiancé about this."

Fern mimed zipping his lips closed. "You can count on me, sweetie. I'm the soul of discretion."

Coming from Georgetown's biggest gossip, this was rich.

"Are you sure you should keep secrets from your fiancé?" Leatrice asked, darting a glance at me as the car bounced over a dip in the cobblestones. "My sugar muffin and I tell each other everything."

"Your sugar muffin isn't a cop," I said. "If you were secretly part of an acting troupe that competed with his business, it might be a different story."

Leatrice tapped her chin. "I never thought of that."

"It's not that I like sneaking around behind Reese's back," I said. "But he has to do everything by the book, and if we wait for things to go through the proper channels, our flowers will be dead and our client's wedding will be ruined."

Kate popped her head between our two seats again. "Nothing

motivates Annabelle like the possibility of a wedding disaster and an unhappy client."

She was right. Not only was an unhappy client bad for business, I couldn't stand the idea of not being able to solve a problem. The urge to fix things seemed to be baked into my DNA.

"I'm with you, sweetie." Catwoman reached up and patted me on the shoulder. "I can't do a bride's hair while she sobs uncontrollably about having no flowers for her wedding. It would stunt my creativity."

"So what's the plan?" Leatrice asked, hooking a left and pumping the brakes as the car dipped down a steep side street.

"The building is around the corner on the right," I said, "but I'd park around here."

Leatrice veered down a narrow alley, and we all sucked in our breath as the car barely missed scraping against one of the brick buildings. She jerked to a stop before hitting a green dumpster.

I braced my hand on the dashboard. "This works." I peered up at the back of the four-story buildings pressed close to each other. "This must be the back of Brianna's building."

"She's on the top floor of one of them," Kate said. "I know it from the front, but they all look the same from back here."

I caught sight of Fern's mask in the rearview mirror. "Maybe we should approach it from the back. That way we won't be seen."

Kate nodded and pointed to the metal stairs clinging to the buildings. "The fire escapes."

Leatrice shuddered. "Again?"

We'd had to hurry down three flights of my rusty fire escape on her wedding day, and I knew it wasn't her fondest memory of the day.

"You should stay here," I told her. "I need you ready to fly when we come out. Just in case we set off alarms or there are guard dogs."

"Guard dogs?" Fern put a hand to his black, leather chest. "Kitty doesn't like dogs."

"I doubt there are dogs," Kate said. "It's Georgetown. Everyone has purse dogs like Hermès. The most they could do would be piddle on your shoes."

I turned and leveled a finger at Fern. "You'll stay outside and be our lookout while Kate and I go inside."

"And how are we getting inside?" Kate asked. "And please don't say bobby pins."

Leatrice held up a wallet-sized leather pouch. "Use my lock-picking set."

I stared at her. "Should I ask where you got this?"

She beamed at me from under the brim of her fedora. "Amazon. They aren't illegal."

"I'll bet using them is," Kate said under her breath.

I reluctantly took the pouch, feeling like I was falling farther down the rabbit hole. "Let's hope we don't need it."

Kate opened her car door. "Let's do this before I come to my senses or lose my nerve."

"We'll be back," I told Leatrice as I followed Kate's lead, joining her and Fern at the bottom of one of the fire escapes. Although the metal stair systems were no longer required for buildings in DC, most of the older buildings still had them, and Georgetown was chock full of old buildings.

"Here goes nothing." Kate clambered up onto the hood of Leatrice's yellow car, then onto the top of the dumpster before climbing the ladder to the first landing of the fire escape.

I followed her, my arms shaking from both nerves and exertion as I pulled myself rung over rung, and Fern brought up the rear. Climbing the stairs was easier, but I was still breathing heavily when we reached the top. Luckily the lights were off in the building, since it wasn't residential and the businesses had closed for the day, so we didn't need to worry about anyone seeing us.

Kate's hands were on her hips as we gathered around the tall windows at the top. "I'm pretty sure this is it."

I squinted to see inside, but all I could see were dark shapes. "I don't see the outlines of branches or bunches of hydrangea, but they could be in another room."

Kate tugged at one of the windows, and it lifted with a groan. "It's open!"

I paused with a hand on her arm, waiting for the sound of an alarm, but none came. "And there's no security system."

"At least not one we can hear," Fern said in a stage whisper, glancing around us as if there was anyone else in the alley to overhear us.

I stole a quick glance down at Leatrice's car, her hat clearly visible through the windshield, and instantly regretted it. Four flights felt a lot higher than it sounded.

Kate pulled the window up all the way and ducked her head inside. "I'm going in."

"Stay out here and keep watch," I told Fern, who nodded solemnly and folded his arms over his chest, before I crawled into the building behind Kate.

When I was inside the room, I paused to let my eyes adjust to the dark. "Where are you?"

"Over here," Kate said.

I tracked her voice to the open door and saw her silhouette appear. We left the room that appeared to be storage, with nothing but a few boxes and a bookshelf, and proceeded down the hall. I heard Kate's shoes tapping on the hardwood floors and realized that even her black boots had heels.

As we approached the front of the building, lights from M Street spilled in through the large windows, and it was easy to see sleek desks against the walls and a large drafting table in the middle of the room. No surprise that even in the dark, the furnishings looked chic and cutting-edge.

"No flowers," Kate said.

Crap. My initial nervousness was replaced with disappointment. If the flowers weren't here, where were they? I was still convinced Brianna had taken them, but now I had no idea where she'd stashed them.

"Now what?" In the shadowy lighting, Kate's face looked fierce as she scanned the office space. "Time for a little payback?"

"No. All I wanted was our flowers. We aren't here for revenge. It's not our style."

"It might be *my* style," Kate mumbled, thumbing through a pile of papers on one of the desks. "You aren't the one whose tires were slashed."

I understood Kate's desire to extract a pound of flesh, but we weren't criminals, despite all current evidence to the contrary.

"Psssst."

I hurried back down the hallway to where Fern's head protruded into the room. "What's up? Is someone coming?"

"I hoped you two were coming," he said. "I'm getting bored out here."

I glanced back to Kate coming down the hall. "There's nothing here. We're ready to go."

Fern held out a hand for both of us as we crawled out the window and slid the glass back down. Despite the fact that we'd come up empty, I was glad we'd managed to get in and out of Brianna's office without anyone being the wiser. Reese would never even need to know about tonight, I thought as I wiped my hands on the front of my black jeans.

"Um, Annabelle," Kate said, leaning over the metal railing. "Where's Leatrice?"

CHAPTER 25

I followed Kate's gaze over the side of the fire escape. Leatrice's car was still in the same place, but even from four stories up, I could see that she was no longer sitting in the driver's side.

"Where could she have gone?" Fern asked. "She was just there a second ago."

I made a quick scan of the alley but didn't see my neighbor's trench-coated figure anywhere. I tuned back to Fern. "You didn't see her leave? Or hear anything suspicious?"

He shook his head, his eyes wide behind his mask. "I did poke my head inside the building when I called for you, but before that, nothing."

My pulse quickened as I started down the escape. "She couldn't have gotten far."

"She wouldn't have wandered off," Kate said, falling in step behind me. "You know she takes her job as wheelman seriously."

That was what scared me. I knew Leatrice wouldn't have walked off. Not when we were relying on her as our getaway driver. At least we weren't in need of a fast getaway.

When I reached the bottom, I descended down the ladder and dropped onto the dumpster.

"Annabelle?"

The muffled voice came from beneath me. I crouched down as Kate landed beside me, her boots making a loud echoing sound on the metal lid.

"I think she's inside the dumpster," I said, holding a hand above me to stop Fern from jumping down.

"What?" Kate dropped to her knees. "Leatrice? Are you in there?"

"Yes, dear. I'm so glad you're back," she said, her voice faint through the steel.

I waved for Fern to join us, then we all hopped from the dumpster onto the hood of the car. We lifted the lid and peeked in. Sure enough, Leatrice stood in the dumpster, along with piles of birch branches and bundles of white hydrangea.

"Our flowers!" Kate nearly dropped her side of the lid as she gaped inside.

I coughed from the putrid scent of garbage and flowers that had been sitting inside a metal box all day, while Fern put a hand over his mouth and gagged.

"Brianna stole them all right," I said. "She just didn't bother schlepping them up to her office."

"She put thousands of dollars worth of imported flowers in a dumpster," Kate said, shaking her head with a hand clamped over her own nose. "Now I'm really sorry we didn't trash her office."

"How did you think to look in here?" I asked my neighbor.

"It was the strangest thing," Leatrice said. "I was sitting in the car waiting for you when this Santa walked up and tapped the top of this dumpster."

Kate exchanged a look with me. "A Santa?"

Leatrice nodded. "I didn't see his face because of the beard and hat, but he made sure to catch my eye before pointing to the dumpster. I got out, but he was running away, so I peeked inside and found all of this. Unfortunately, the lid was too heavy for me to hold up and I leaned over too far."

"Brilliant, sweetie," Fern said, through his hand. "Too bad we're going to have to wash you in tomato juice to get rid of this smell."

"Are you okay?" I asked.

She nodded with a smile. "Just fine, dear. The flowers cushioned my fall."

"At least she found them," I said under my breath to myself as much as to anyone, as Fern and I held out hands to pull her out.

"I think you mean Santa found them," Kate muttered.

I was pretty sure Leatrice didn't hallucinate seeing Santa, but why was someone dressed up as Santa creeping around Georgetown at night, and how had they known something was in the dumpster? Something we were there to find? My first instinct was that it had been Kris, but his Santa suit was still with the cops. Of course, he could have gotten a new one, but just how many Santa suits were floating around in the city for everyone to be turning up in one?

Leatrice passed us a bundle of branches wrapped in brown paper. "Let me hand you the flowers before you pull me up."

Kate took the bundle and jumped down from the hood. "We can put these in the trunk."

"I told Buster and Mack that I'd call them if we found the flowers," I said. "They can bring their van."

"Do you really want to hang out in the alley any longer than we need to?" Kate asked as she leaned into Leatrice's car and popped the trunk. "Besides, have you seen how big this trunk is?"

Knowing the overall dimensions of the old car, I suspected it was sizable. "Okay. I guess the flowers can't get banged up any more than they already have."

The branches looked fine, although the hydrangea looked danger-ously wilted. I hoped Buster and Mack could work their magic on them.

Leatrice handed up another bundle, followed by a tightly wrapped cluster of hydrangea. I handed them down to Kate, who proceeded to put them in the trunk. After a few minutes, Leatrice was passing up the last of the flowers, and then Fern and I were hauling her out.

We both stepped back once we'd deposited her onto the hood of her car and let the heavy, metal lid slam shut. The scent of the dump-ster seemed to linger even though she was outside, and I suspected it had permeated her clothes. None of us probably smelled great at this point.

"Are you sure it was Santa you saw?" I asked Leatrice. "Not just someone in red and white. The lighting isn't great back here."

Leatrice looked askance at me. "I know my Santas, dear. He was in the full suit--shiny belt, white beard, and all."

Kate shrugged at me. "Looks like we're the only people not wearing a Santa suit around here. I mean, it is December."

"Did my lock-picking kit work upstairs?" Leatrice asked once we'd all gotten off her hood and into the car. A few bundles of flowers that hadn't fit in the trunk were stacked up between Kate and Fern in the back seat, and Fern had his window open and his head out.

"We didn't need to use it," I said. "The window was open."

"That was lucky. So you didn't leave any trace that you'd been there?" Leatrice reached over and patted my hand. "I knew you'd be a natural."

Although Leatrice thought she was paying me a compliment, I really didn't want to be a natural at breaking and entering. "I'm just grateful we have the flowers back."

"I'm texting Buster and Mack to tell them we're on the way," Kate said, tapping away on her phone in the back seat. "They're going to need to make room in their cooler."

"They have a cooler in their floral shop?" Leatrice asked, twisting around as she started the car and put it in reverse.

"A big one," Kate said. "I've had smaller apartments than their floral cooler."

Leatrice accelerated backward, slamming on the brakes when we reached the street. "Anyone coming?"

Fern poked his head out farther, swinging it from side to side. "Nope. You're all clear."

Leatrice pulled the car out backward, barely missing a car parked too close to the alleyway entrance before turning back onto the steep street leading toward the river. "In and out and no one saw us."

"Rock on wood," Kate said.

Leatrice cocked her head, mouthing the phrase to herself.

"She means 'knock on wood,'" I whispered.

"Can we please talk about the fact that one of our wedding planning colleagues stole a flower order and dumped it in the garbage?" Kate said. "I know we've had friendly competitors before, but this is getting out of hand."

I agreed with Kate, but from watching Reese put together his cases, I knew proving our accusations would be difficult. "I don't know what we can actually do."

"I have some ideas," Kate said.

"That we can do legally," I clarified.

Kate leaned forward. "Now you want to keep things legal?"

I pointed to an intersection ahead. "We're going to make a right up there, Leatrice."

"Obviously, the rumors about Brianna being a call girl weren't upsetting enough," Fern said. "What if we tell people she's a Russian spy?"

"Getting her shipped off to Moscow would be good," Kate said.

I sighed as I turned to face the back seat. "We're not going to accuse someone of being a traitor, even if she deserves it."

"Wrong street, Leatrice," Kate said, looking over my shoulder and out the front windshield.

"Oops." Leatrice giggled. "I'll just swing in here and then back us up."

"Besides," I said, "we don't know anyone who could ship Brianna off to Russia."

Kate gave me a sinister smile. "Speak for yourself. I'm pretty sure one of the guys I dated last year was CIA. You know when they say they're State Department, but are vague about specifics, that they're actually CIA."

Leatrice pumped the brakes and twisted her head around. "Is that true?"

I shook my head as Kate bobbed hers up and down vigorously.

"What's that all about?" Fern asked, lifting his cat mask and leaning forward to peer past me.

I spun back around and saw that we'd turned down another narrow alley, this one filled with a pair of box trucks and a bunch of thick-necked guys unloading them into a building. When they saw our car, one of the men started taking long steps toward us.

"Uh oh," Leatrice said, as the man's jacket flapped open revealing a gun in a holster.

"Get us out of here," I told her, sliding down in the passenger's seat. "Fast."

CHAPTER 26

"Is he still chasing us?" I asked, craning my neck to peek into the back seat.

Fern popped his head out his window, then ducked back inside. "No sign of him."

"Keep driving," I told Leatrice, waving one hand at the street. "We should go the back way to Lush."

Leatrice nodded, her hands clutched tightly around the steering wheel that seemed to dwarf her. "Goodness me. Wasn't that exciting?"

"Which part?" Kate asked, sinking into the beige, velour upholstery. "It's been a busy night."

The air coming into the car from the open windows was cool, and I hoped that meant the heat wave was breaking. I also hoped the air could help dissipate some of the lingering aroma of garbage. It was bad enough that the back seat was piled high with wilting flowers. As delicately perfumed as flowers were when they were fresh, they smelled awful once they started to wilt.

Leatrice flicked her eyes to the rearview mirror. "Why do you think that gentleman was chasing our car? You don't think he knew what we were up to, do you?"

"Doubtful," I said, putting a hand to my heart and feeling it hammer away. "I think he was afraid we'd see what he and his pals were up to."

Kate pulled her black cap off and ran a hand through her hair. "You think something criminal was going on?"

"Why else unload stuff in the middle of the night and have a bunch of neckless guys with guns doing it?" I asked.

"Maybe because it's impossible to park in Georgetown during the day?" Fern said. "I know I despise delivery trucks blocking the road during rush hour. I wouldn't mind a few more making deliveries in the evening."

"I'd say it's later than 'evening.'" I glanced down at the simulated wood dashboard of Leatrice's car before realizing there was no clock, just knobs to tune the radio and small levers to adjust the air conditioning. There wasn't a single digital thing in the car. Not shocking considering she'd probably purchased it during the Reagan administration.

"Who makes deliveries at midnight?" Kate said, clearing up my question of what time it was.

"Spies," Leatrice said in a hushed voice, tipping her slightly stained fedora back on her head. "I always knew Georgetown was a hotbed of spy activity, but who knew how much crime went on around here at night?"

"Makes you glad you live with a cop, right?" Kate asked.

"Yes," Leatrice answered, bobbing her head up and down.

I pointed to a street ahead of us. "Turn here."

"Scary guys aside, does anyone think the Santa who tipped us off about the flowers might have been Kris?" Kate asked, as Leatrice made the turn, and she and Fern slid to one side of the car.

"Possibly," I said. "There's no way to know for sure since Leatrice didn't get a good look at his face."

"And he wasn't singing," Leatrice said. "I would have recognized the singing."

"We could ask Kris," Fern said.

I spun around to face him. "Are you telling me you know he's alive and you know where to find him, because if you've been keeping this from me and from Reese then--"

LAURA DURHAM

"Unclench, sweetie," Fern said with a loud exhale. "I'm not saying any of that. I did, however, leave the key to my storage room over the sill in case Kris needed a place to sleep. I also left out some Christmas cookies."

"He's not *actually* Santa," Kate said.

"I know that." Fern straightened his cat mask. "It's not like I left out reindeer food, too."

"Reindeer food?" Leatrice shook her head. "What will you kids think of next?"

"I could always leave a note in case it's really him," Fern continued. "Maybe he'd be willing to talk to us."

"What if it's not him?" I asked. "What if it's Stanley?"

Fern ran his fingers down his long whiskers. "Then he won't answer. Can't hurt to try."

As much as I hated to admit it, leaving a note out for fake Santa Claus was the best option we had at the moment. Even thought I'd promised not to get sucked into the case--and meant it--I also wanted to see Kris Kringle back singing. If it couldn't feel like Christmas yet, at least it could sound like it.

I pointed to a barely visible driveway. "We'll go into this alley behind the shop to unload."

"Another alley?" Fern asked. "I'm starting to have post traumatic stress at the mention of alleys."

"This one should be safe," I said, holding the door handle again as Leatrice swung the car wide to make the tight turn. "Besides, Buster and Mack will be waiting for us."

Fern let out a dramatic sigh. "Good. We should really bring our biker gang muscle with us more often."

Not a bad plan, until people realized our friends were with a *Christian* biker gang and their answer to most problems was a prayer chain.

"Nothing happened," I reminded everyone. "We didn't damage Brianna's office; we found the flowers, and we hightailed it away from the scary guys in the alley. I'd call tonight a success."

"We might have seen something illegal going down." Leatrice slowed as we drove down the narrow alleyway. "Are you sure we shouldn't call your fiancé and tell him?"

146

"No," I said a little too forcefully. "He pulled a double shift, so I don't want to wake him."

The real reason was that I didn't want to explain why we were dressed in black from head to foot, and in Fern's case, mask. As sympathetic as I knew he'd be to our flower crisis, those feelings wouldn't extend to breaking and entering, although technically we'd only done one of those things. Telling him we might have happened upon a connection to the Kris Kringle Jingle case might make him think we'd been looking for it, which we hadn't, but he seemed to be skeptical of coincidence.

"Suit yourself," Kate said, "but you know he'll find out sooner or later. The man's like a human polygraph machine."

Leatrice pulled to a stop, and I spotted Buster and Mack standing at the back entrance to their shop. I knew they often burned the midnight oil, so I didn't feel bad about having them meet us so late.

"I can't believe it," Mack said, rushing over as we got out of the car. "You found our flowers."

"In a dumpster?" Buster asked, shaking his head as if he couldn't quite believe it. "How did you know to search dumpsters?"

"We didn't actually search dumpsters," I said. "Someone dressed as Santa tipped off Leatrice."

"Then I fell in," she said with a giggle. "I'm glad these three finished breaking into that wedding planner's office and found me. It was getting awfully stuffy in there."

Mack's mouth fell open. "A Santa? Was it Kris?"

"Leatrice couldn't tell," I said. "We didn't break in, by the way. We merely had a look around. Her office happened to be open."

Fern held up a finger. "Office window."

I shot him a look. "Cat burglars never tell their secrets."

Buster peered into the back seat, inhaling sharply when he saw the bundles of wilted flowers wrapped in brown paper. "We'd better get these hydrangea in water."

Kate opened the trunk and waved a hand at the birch branches. "Voila. Your winter wonderland."

Mack lumbered around to stand next to her. "I can't believe it. We were about to start gathering fallen branches and paint them with streaks of white."

Kate wrinkled her nose. "We would have had to turn the lights very low to make that work."

Buster filled his arms with flowers. "I'm glad you're all safe. Mack and I activated our emergency prayer chain this evening. You've had dozens of Road Riders for Jesus sending up messages for you."

"We weren't specific, of course," Mack added.

"Well whatever you did worked," I said. "Not only did we find the flowers, Leatrice might have spotted Kris, and we possibly witnessed some criminal activity."

"In addition to our own," Kate said, stacking the branches high in Mack's outstretched arms.

"I don't suppose you feel like sharing that with the police?" Mack asked, peering over the branches at an unmarked car driving down the alley toward us, the portable light on its roof flashing.

I swallowed hard as I looked at my crew--Leatrice dressed like a vintage spy, Fern in a Catwoman costume, and Kate and I in black from head to toe. This was going to be a tough one to explain.

"What a relief," Leatrice said as the officer stepped out of the car. "It's Reese."

I almost groaned out loud.

CHAPTER 27

"I know you're mad at me," I said, as Reese and I trudged up the last few steps to our apartment. "You've barely spoken to me since we left Buster and Mack's, and you won't hold my hand."

He flicked a glance at me as he opened the front door and held it open for me. "Babe, you smell like a garbage truck, and your hands are filthy."

I raised an arm to smell my shirt and cringed from the pungent smell as I walked inside ahead of him. "That may be true, but that doesn't mean you're not upset at me."

"Upset?" He tossed his keys on top of the bookshelf by the door. "Why would I be upset? I only came home from a really crappy day to find you gone and your phone on the coffee table. Then that phone starts blowing up with concerned texts from Mack about your covert mission, and when I come to find you, I see you and your cohorts dressed like you stepped out of a bad spy movie mixed with a really bad superhero movie."

I was glad Fern wasn't there to hear that. He took great offense when someone implied his outfits weren't authentic.

"How did you find me, anyway?" I picked up my phone from the glass coffee table and saw the series of increasingly hysterical messages from Mack scrolling down the locked screen. "You couldn't use the 'Find My Friends' app since my phone wasn't on me."

He cocked an eyebrow at me. "You think your phone is the only one I track?"

I wasn't sure if I should be disturbed or relieved that my fiancé kept tabs on my friends, too.

"I'm sorry I didn't leave a note," I said. Not that I knew what that note would have said. *Off to break into someone's office and rescue our stolen flowers* didn't seem like it would have made the situation any better. I was sorrier that I'd left my phone behind.

He went into the kitchen, and I could hear him opening the refrigerator. When he returned, he handed me one of his beers with the cap already twisted off. "I know you're not a beer drinker, but you probably need this."

"Thanks." I took a tentative swig of the microbrew, trying not to make a face as I swallowed. Nope. Still not a beer person.

"You want to tell me why you all smelled like you'd been rooting around in a landfill?"

I'd managed to avoid telling Reese the entire story when he'd arrived to find us behind Lush, partly because I knew having Leatrice and Fern around during the retelling would not help my case, and partly because I'd been so relieved to see him after the stressful evening that I'd wanted to do nothing more than go home.

"The long and short of it is that one of our unfriendly competitors stole the floral order for this weekend's wedding, and we found it in a dumpster behind her office building. Actually, someone dressed as Santa tipped off Leatrice, and then she found it by falling into a dumpster. It took all of us to get the flowers--and Leatrice--out and loaded into her car, and they smelled pretty bad after sitting in a big, metal container all day." I took another drink of the beer, wishing it was one of the crisp sauvignon blancs Richard preferred and often stocked in my refrigerator. "So, if you think about it, we were merely righting a wrong."

"Did you say Santa tipped her off?"

"I know," I said. "More Santas. There must be a sale on Santa suits somewhere. We don't know if it was Kris or not. Leatrice couldn't tell, but if it was, he got his hands on a new suit."

"Speaking of that, I heard back from the lab about Kris's bloody costume." He paused to tip back his beer. "It wasn't human blood."

"Not human?" I ran a hand through my hair and got another unpleasant whiff of garbage. I needed a shower.

"It was bovine."

"Cow's blood." I made a face. "How do you get that?"

"Butcher's shop? Grocery store meat department? Restaurant kitchen?" Reese suggested. "I'm sure someone living on the streets would know where to source it."

"That doesn't happen by accident," I said. "So it was staged to look like he was hurt or killed?"

"Looks like it."

"That explains Fern's storage room and Jeannie being so confident her friend wasn't dead. He's not," I said.

"But he wanted someone to think he was." Reese took another long pull from his beer. "It feels like someone's trying to make a point with all the Santas, and maybe that someone is Kris."

"You think Kris Kringle Jingle staged his own murder and is now running around framing criminals and dressing them up as Santa?" I asked, thinking it didn't sound like such a crazy idea once I'd said it out loud. "That means Stanley isn't a killer on the run. Then why is he still missing?"

"Maybe he knew about Kris staging his death."

I snapped my fingers. "Because he planted the suit. But why disappear?"

"Everyone who seems to know something about Kris's disappearance has gone underground. They must think that knowing about it puts them at risk."

"At risk from whom?" I started pacing a small circle. "If Stanley isn't a killer and the other Santas didn't knock him off, then we're back to whatever it was he saw. And what's up with all the Santa-related crimes?"

"Richard was right when he said the holidays make people crazy." He folded his arms over his broad chest. "Speaking of crazy, do you want to explain what you and your motley crew were wearing tonight?"

I considered not mentioning our little expedition inside Brianna's office an omission and not a lie. Besides, we hadn't *broken* in, although we'd been intending to. "We didn't want to stick out while we searched for the flowers. We thought all black would make us blend in."

"If you wanted to blend in, you shouldn't have taken Fern or Leatrice," he muttered from behind his beer.

"Believe me, it wasn't our plan to bring them." I set my nearly full bottle on the coffee table and headed down the hall, pulling off my shirt as I walked. "But you know how hard it is to get out without Leatrice seeing you."

"I've considered rappelling before," Reese said, watching me disappear into the bathroom.

I laughed as I peeled off the rest of my clothes and turned on the shower. "Our neighbors would love that."

Reese appeared in the open bathroom door as I stepped into the shower and pulled the curtain closed. "If you're right about this Brianna being the one to threaten you, then pop Kate's tires and steal Buster and Mack's flowers, it seems like she's escalating pretty quickly."

"Do you think we should press charges?"

"Maybe if you hadn't taken the evidence out of the dumpster behind her offices," he said. "But now it might be tough to prove anything."

I let the water pour over me and hopefully wash away any trace of rancid flowers. "If we'd left them any longer, there would have been no chance to save them. As it is, they're not in great shape, but hopefully Buster and Mack can nurse them back to health in time for Saturday. I'll have to find a different way to deal with Brianna."

"I hope that doesn't mean taking things into your own hands and going vigilante."

"Do I strike you as the vigilante type?" I asked, as the warm water pounded against the knots in my shoulders.

"I was thinking more about Kate," he said.

"I can't make any promises when it comes to Kate. She did suggest having Brianna shipped off to Siberia. I'm pretty sure she can't actually pull it off, though."

"You're only pretty sure?"

I poured some coconut-scented shower gel into my hands and lathered it over my body. "She has a lot of ex-boyfriends in the government. I make no promises. Usually it comes in handy, like when we need to get special permits for elephants parading down Constitution Avenue or group tickets for tours of the Capitol."

He chuckled. "I hope your clients appreciate everything you two do for them, babe."

I poked my head out of the curtain. "If we do our jobs well, they'll never know any of this ever happened."

"And this other planner has no idea you rescued the flowers?"

I turned off the water. "Nope. No one saw us getting the flowers out of the dumpster. The alley was deserted. Aside from Santa." I hesitated as I pulled back the curtain, wondering whether or not to mention what we'd seen when we'd inadvertently driven down the wrong alley. I decided since I was busted, I might as well. "But we were spotted by some unsavory characters when we were driving to Lush."

"There are a lot of unsavory characters late at night in Georgetown," Reese said, handing me a towel.

I wrapped the towel around my chest then grabbed another for my hair. "Yeah, but these guys had guns, and one chased our car out of the alley."

He frowned. "You were chased at gunpoint and you're just now mentioning it?"

I flipped my head over and twisted the second towel around my wet hair, flipping it up and making it into a turban. "It's been a pretty busy night. Besides, it happened pretty fast, and Leatrice got us out of there before anything happened." I let out a breath. "I knew if I told you we saw something suspicious, you'd assume we were meddling in the case, which I promise you we're not."

My fiancé dragged a hand through his hair. "The case?"

"Kris Kringle Jingle said he saw something suspicious in George-town, and then he disappeared. What if we saw the same thing?"

He opened his mouth as if to argue with me, then clamped it closed. He dragged a hand through his hair. "How do you and your friends manage to stumble into crimes wherever you go?"

"I honestly don't know."

He shook his head. "It's really hard to stay angry at you when you're wearing nothing but a towel." He took another steadying breath. "Okay. Where did this happen?"

I thought back to the street we'd accidentally turned onto. "An alley down near the water. I think it was off of Thirty-first." I took a step closer. "Are you saying you think my hunch might be right?"

He narrowed his eyes at me. "I'm only saying it might be worth checking out."

"Can you investigate if there's not an official report or request?"

Reese wrapped an arm around me and pulled me close. "You're not the only one who can follow a hunch and disobey orders."

My pulse quickened as his hazel eyes deepened to green. I loved it when he talked dirty.

CHAPTER 28

"So he's going rogue?" Kate asked, as we stood at the back of Western Presbyterian Church the next evening.

"Not exactly," I said. "But he's going to poke around off the books."

Kate nudged me. "I think we're rubbing off on him."

"I don't know if that's a good thing or not."

After a hectic week, we'd both taken the day off to prepare for the weekend's wedding, and now we were waiting for the bridal party to arrive for the ceremony rehearsal. As usual, we were early, and, as it was with most rehearsals, the bridal party was late.

The church was lit at the front of the sanctuary, the light wood wainscoting and carved wooden arch overhead illuminated with lights behind the choir loft. It was already dark outside, so the stained glass windows along both sides of the church were muted, although the hanging pendant lamps over the pews shone down.

"It could have been anything, you know." Kate walked from the church foyer into the sanctuary, stepping on the wine-colored carpeting that ran down the center aisle. "Just because the guy had a gun, doesn't mean he's a criminal. Half the people in the country are packing, and some of them walk around with semiautomatics strapped to their backs just because they can. Of course, if you ask me, those guys are compensating for something."

I glanced around the quiet church, hoping a minister wasn't within earshot. "You're right. It could have been a regular, law-abiding citizen who just happened to be unloading a truck of perfectly legal goods in the dead of night."

Kate smirked at me. "Well, when you say it like that, it sounds silly."

I breathed in the scent of lilies, noticing two aging arrangements of white blooms at the altar. I knew Buster and Mack would be replacing those with their own stunning arrangements of blooming branches and hydrangea—as long as the flowers had sufficiently recovered. If anyone could pull off a wedding miracle, it was my florists with the super-charged prayer chain and faith as expansive as their biceps.

"I'm going to go look for the minister," I said, with a glance at my phone. "It's one thing for the bride and groom to be late, but we can't start rehearsing without her."

"Don't leave me here." Kate hurried behind me as I started to walk up one side of the sanctuary.

I looked back at her. "It's a church. I think you're safe."

She rubbed her arms. "Empty churches feel spooky, and they echo too much."

I shook my head as we snaked our way through the sanctuary and along a corridor to the administrative building attached to the church. It was quiet here, too. No doubt, the staff had all left early for the weekend.

"I don't see her," Kate said, sticking close to me as we continued down a softly lit hallway.

I found the minister's office, but the door was locked and the lights were off. So much for that. "You called and confirmed the rehearsal time, right?"

Kate bobbed her head up and down. "I talked to the reverend herself. Confirmed the time and date. I'm sure that's why the sanctuary is open and the lights are on."

She was right about that. If there wasn't anything going on in the sanctuary, the front doors would not have been unlocked for us.

"Where could she be?" I asked. "I know we're early, but this thing is supposed to start in fifteen minutes. The entire church is deserted."

"Not the *entire* church. There's Miriam's Kitchen."

"Miriam's Kitchen? You mean the soup kitchen?"

Kate let out an impatient breath. "It's a bit more than that, and it's inside the church."

I pointed to the floor. "This church?" How had I not known that? Although, to be fair, Kate had done all the work coordinating with the church on this wedding.

More nods from my assistant. "Yep. I think it's still open for a little while longer."

"Maybe the reverend is there," I suggested, heading off down the hall again.

Kate caught my arm and tugged me in the other direction. "This way, boss."

She led me through the church and outside. We walked down the side of the stone building to a stone arch with iron gates standing open.

"How do you know about this?" I asked.

"I came here to drop off the couple's application, remember?" She smiled as she ducked past the gates. "I got a full tour."

I followed her into a large room that had fluorescent lighting running overhead and reminded me a bit of the other shelter we'd visited, although this one had paper snowflakes hanging down from the ceiling. The tables were round instead of rectangular, circled with gray, metal folding chairs. The room was warm and smelled like food, the lingering scent of lunch and coffee hanging in the air.

It was clear that Miriam's Kitchen was preparing to close for the evening. Only a few people were scattered around the tables, but my gaze faltered when I saw one figure crouched over a far table.

"No reverend," Kate said with a sigh.

I nudged her and pointed to the man in red and white. "But we found another Santa."

"You don't think it's . . .?" Her words trailed off.

"What are the chances of us finding Kris at a shelter all the way across town that happens to be in our bride's church?" I asked as I led the way through the tables toward the man, my heart pounding.

He looked up as we approached, and my heart sank.

"Apparently, not great," Kate said, sounding as defeated as I was.

It wasn't Kris. This man was gaunt with dark circles under his eyes and had none of the merry twinkle that the singing Santa did.

"You're not Kris," I said to answer the questioning look in his eyes.

His face contorted for a moment, and he shook his head vigorously. "Nope."

I watched his cheeks color beneath the gray stubble covering them. "Are you Stanley?"

He rubbed his nose and answered quickly. "Nope."

"Now, why are you lying to these nice ladies?" A burly man with thick arms and a deep baritone voice asked as he wiped off a table nearby.

Kate and I both turned to the man who wore a white apron over his T-shirt.

"This is Stanley?" Kate asked, jerking a thumb toward the Santa squirming in his chair.

"He sure is." The man with the apron gave us a wide smile as he walked back toward the kitchen. The clattering of pans told me there were more people cleaning up back there.

I pivoted to face Stanley, who'd scooted a few chairs away from us. "We're not here to turn you in."

He blanched. "Why would you turn me in? I haven't done nothing wrong." He looked from me to Kate. "Who are you?"

I thought for a second about the best way to sell ourselves. "We're friends with Buster and Mack."

His face relaxed a little bit. "Why are you here?"

"Believe it or not," Kate said, putting her hands on her hips. "It's a total coincidence. We're running a wedding rehearsal here."

"A lot of people have been looking for you," I said. "People are worried about you."

He gave a snort. "I'll bet folks have been looking for me."

"We know Kris isn't dead," I said, hoping I was right and hoping this would get him to talk.

He pressed his lips together. "You don't know nothing."

"Why are you dressed up like Santa?" Kate asked. "Taking over your friend's beat?"

Stanley shook his head. "It's not like that."

"Tell us then," I said. "Whatever's going on, we'd like to help."

"She's engaged to a cop," Kate said. "If you need protection, I'm sure Annabelle can arrange it."

Another derisive laugh. "You two are in over your heads."

"Always a possibility," Kate muttered, pulling her phone out of her purse as it vibrated. She elbowed me, and I glanced over at the text. The bride had arrived and now *she* was the only person in the sanctuary. From the liberal use of exclamation marks, she wasn't taking it in stride.

"We'd like to talk to you more . . ." I began as I turned back to Stanley.

"That was fast," Kate said, twisting around to take in the now-empty room.

Stanley was gone.

CHAPTER 29

I surveyed the rehearsal dinner space with my hands on my hips as waiters scurried around filling water glasses and lighting candles.

"No mentioning any of this to Richard," I warned Kate.

She nodded, fluffing a faux burlap linen on a high-top table. "You mean the homeless Santa who might or might not have something to do with Kris Kringle Jingle, who might or might not be dead?"

I let out a steadying breath. "Yes, that."

We'd made a cursory attempt to find Stanley, but he'd ducked out through the kitchen and disappeared into the night. After that, we'd been focused on calming the bride and getting the rehearsal going. The reverend had arrived late, as well as the church wedding coordinator, and Kate and I had been able to race over to the rehearsal dinner venue ahead of the bridal party.

Kate mimed zipping her lips. "The secret is safe with me."

Richard came up behind us with an electric lighter in one hand. "What are we keeping secret now?"

I put a hand to my heart. "Don't sneak up on me like that. You scared me half to death."

Richard eyed me. "A little jumpy, darling?"

"Just excited to put this weekend in the rearview mirror." I turned to him as Kate stepped away to fluff more linens. "It looks great."

We'd ducked out of the wedding rehearsal at the church--after lining up the processional and being shooed out by the rather territorial church lady--and rushed over to the Dockmaster Building at the DC Wharf. The two-story space perched on the end of the long dock and had three walls of floor-to-ceiling glass, giving it wide views of the Potomac River and a distant view of the monuments. When we'd booked it for December, we'd never imagined being able to use the balcony, but I noticed high tables scattered near the glass railing that ringed the second level.

Even though it didn't feel wintery outside, the après ski lodge decor made the inside look as cozy as a chalet in Aspen. A fake fur runner ran down the middle of both long dinner tables, topped with glass-encased pillar candles and freestanding antlers. A bar made with frosted logs sat off to the side with evergreens towering behind it, and chic brown leather furniture groupings were positioned on either side of the tables, cashmere throws draped over the love seats. The room even smelled like a Christmas tree.

"You'd never know it's T-shirt weather outside," I said.

Richard frowned, giving my sleeveless black dress a quick once-over. "You could have dressed more to the theme."

I noticed that he wore tweed and wondered how he wasn't sweating bullets. "I don't own anything that screams ski lodge in summer."

He sniffed and arched a brow. "More's the pity. I have the AC cranked as high as it will go, so you might be wishing for a sweater soon."

"None of the guests are dressed for cold weather," I reminded him. "Do you really want people shivering their way through dinner?"

"That's what the throws are for." He waved to the clear chivari chairs around the dinner tables, and I noticed cream-and-brown plaid pashminas draped over the backs.

Leave it to Richard to create a practical problem and solve it in the most stylish way.

"I checked the weather app," I said, holding up my phone. "The temperature is supposed to drop tonight."

Richard sniffed. "A lot of good that does me."

"Well, it makes the wedding reception a bit less ridiculous." I tucked my phone back into my dress pocket, as I spotted the event photographer leaning close to a place setting and snapping away. "And no one can tell how cold it was in photos."

Richard tapped a finger to his jaw. "You make a good point. This will still look fabulous on the Richard Gerard website."

"See? Lemonade out of lemons."

"I would love some lemonade," Fern said, dashing across the room from the entrance and wheeling his small black suitcase of hair supplies behind him. "It's perfect lemonade weather."

Richard scowled at him and I glanced around quickly, hoping he didn't have Leatrice in tow. Sometimes Leatrice manages to sweet-talk her way into my weddings, and Fern was usually the softest mark.

"What are you doing here?" I asked.

He fluttered a hand at me. "The bride wanted me to meet her here for touch-ups after the rehearsal."

Kate walked back up. "She needs touch-ups already? Didn't you just do her hair an hour ago?"

Fern shrugged. "I don't ask questions, sweetie. I just nod and smile."

Not a bad policy for working with brides.

"How did the rehearsal at the church go?" Fern asked, touching a hand to his low ponytail. "I tried to calm her down at the hotel when she was getting ready."

"Not bad," I said. "She was a little nervous when she got there, but by the time we lined up the bridal party, she seemed more relaxed."

"That's because I gave her some wine," Kate said.

"Wine?" I looked at her. "When? Where?"

"In the holding room at the back of the church while you were talking to the reverend."

My stomach tightened. "Where did you get the wine?" I wouldn't have put it past her to carry travel-sized bottles with her, but I suspected this wasn't the case.

"It was in the holding room," she said. "I didn't give her much. Just enough to take the edge off."

Richard stared at her. "You gave the bride sacramental wine?"

Even though he considered himself a lapsed Catholic, I could see a swoon coming.

"Let's just be glad the bride is happy and calm and in a good mood," I said, taking Richard's arm. "We like happy clients, right?"

"Of course," he muttered, still goggling at Kate.

"And she'll never know she almost had a floral-free wedding," Fern said, with a giggle that made me wonder if he'd gotten into some wine somewhere. "No amount of church wine could fix that."

Richard swung his attention to Fern. "What do you mean?"

Fern's eyes grew wide as the realization hit him that he'd get to share a juicy tidbit of gossip. "Didn't you hear? That Botoxed Barbie wedding planner made off with the flowers for the reception tomorrow, and we rescued them from a dumpster."

I closed my eyes for a moment, bracing for Richard's reaction.

"I beg your pardon?" he said, his voice eerily calm.

"It was so thrilling," Fern continued as Kate shook her head furtively. "I was the lookout while Annabelle and Kate looked for the flowers in Brianna's office, and Leatrice was the wheelman. Or wheellady, to be more accurate."

Richard pivoted his head to me. "Annabelle?"

"To be fair, you warned me not to meddle in the murder investigation. This had nothing to do with any murder or any of Reese's investigations."

"I thought it went unsaid that you shouldn't break into your competitor's office."

"First of all," Kate said, holding up a finger, "we didn't break in. She left her window open. And second, you would have done the same thing if your top rival had stolen all the food for one of your parties."

He opened his mouth, then paused. "You're right, although I might have done it in broad daylight so I couldn't be accused of subterfuge. What if she'd caught you?"

"Well, you don't have to worry," I said. "No one saw us and we didn't leave a trace that we'd been there. We didn't even touch anything. There's no way she'll ever know we were snooping around."

"She's going to know you got the flowers back," Richard said, holding up his phone. "Unless you plan not to post any photos from the wedding day."

I groaned and looked at the pained expression on Kate's face. "We could survive not posting any Instagram stories of this wedding, right?"

She gnawed on her lower lip. "But our brides love it when we post about their weddings and use their custom wedding hashtag."

"If you don't post, someone will," Fern said. "You can't have a social media blackout on the wedding."

He was right. As soon as a post went up with the wedding flowers in it, Brianna would know we'd been scrounging around in her dumpster.

"At least she won't know we were in her office," I said, although I suspected she would not be pleased that her plans to ruin our wedding were foiled.

Richard shrugged. "Unless she has security cameras."

I swallowed hard. I hadn't thought about that, since we didn't have a security system in Wedding Belles HQ, aka my apartment. But a wedding planner bankrolled by her rich father might very well have cameras in her office. From the stricken look on Kate's face, I could tell she was thinking the same thing.

Fern took Richard's hand and patted it. "That's enough helping from you, sweetie."

CHAPTER 30

"No, I don't think she's going to come after us while we're sleeping," I told Kate over the phone as I walked toward my apartment building. I saw a quick flash of a man in a hoodie and glasses leaving the building, so I ran to catch the door, glancing back at the slim figure and wondering if he was a new neighbor. I knew I'd seen him before. "We don't know she has cameras in her office space."

Kate let out a breath. "That's true."

I trudged up the stairs and paused at the door to my apartment. Not a comforting thought since Reese was still at work. "Just lock your doors and park your car someplace safe."

"Oh, I'm not staying at my place tonight," she said. "It's too hot."

"Hot?" The weather had finally dipped down, and there had been a chill in the air when we'd left the Dockmaster's Building.

"You know, dangerous. I'm going to stay someplace else until things cool off."

I rolled my eyes and was glad she couldn't see me. Our recent encounter with a few members of the mob had definitely made an impression on Kate. "Do I want to ask where you're staying?"

"Let's just say, I'll be very safe."

My money was on her bunking with one of her exes who was

potentially CIA or the firefighter she'd gone out with a few times after my car had been burned to the ground by a Molotov cocktail. "Don't forget we start bright and early tomorrow at the Four Seasons."

"I still don't get why we have to be there for hair and makeup," she grumbled. "All we do is sit and watch the bridal party get ready."

"Because it's better than being at home and getting hundreds of texts and calls from the nervous bride. Our presence is like a comfort blanket, and it usually keeps them from going off the rails."

"If you say so, boss." There was a second, deeper voice in the background. "I'll see you tomorrow."

She clicked off, and I slipped my phone into my dress pocket. At least I didn't need to worry about Brianna coming after Kate tonight. Reese was right. The woman was escalating, and I didn't trust her not to do something crazy.

I opened my door, hesitating before going inside. Had I left the lights on? The living room was fully illuminated, making me wonder if Reese had gotten off earlier. I called his name, but the only response was Hermès scampering up and sniffing my ankles.

Okay, I knew I didn't have a dog in my apartment when I left. "Leatrice?"

My petite neighbor bounded down the hall, her black Mary Tyler Moore flip bouncing. "I'm so glad you're home. We've been too scared to go back downstairs."

I glanced back at the completely quiet stairwell then back at my neighbor in her brown footie pajamas with bear ears. "Scared of what?"

Leatrice didn't answer but instead, turned around and called behind her, "It's okay, honeybun. It's just Annabelle."

Honeybun, aka Sidney Allen, appeared from the far end of the hall. He was almost as petite as his wife, but with much less hair. Where Leatrice was all bones with skin that hung off her like flesh-colored chiffon, the entertainment diva was shaped like an egg with no discernible waist. He almost always wore a dark suit with the pants hiked up nearly to his armpits, and his thinning hair seemed to have a perpetual crease from the headset he wore when he was coordinating his performers at an event. This evening there was no headset, and burgundy velvet pajamas replaced the suit, but the elastic pants were tugged up nearly to his chin.

"Hello, Annabelle," he said in his gentlemanly Southern drawl, as if him padding down my hallway in his PJs was the most normal thing in the world.

"Were you in our bed?" I asked, wondering if I was going to need to get new sheets or move.

Leatrice giggled. "Don't be silly, dear. My sugar muffin was heading down the fire escape."

I shut the door behind me. "What's going on? Why are you going down the fire escape in your pajamas?"

"Because of the men who tried to get into our apartment," Sidney Allen said.

I looked at Leatrice, who was bobbing her head up and down. "What men?"

"Well, if we knew who they were we wouldn't be running from them, now would we?" Leatrice shook her head at me. "We'd just turned on Perry Mason when we heard someone jiggling the front door."

"We had the lights off," Sidney Allen said, "so they may have assumed we weren't home."

"Wouldn't they have heard *Perry Mason*?" I asked.

Leatrice blushed. "We were watching the TV in the bedroom. It's the fancy flat screen my sweetie pie brought over from his place."

"Okay. So you heard someone trying to get in your front door," I prompted. "And then what?"

"We ran out and turned on the lights," Leatrice said. "I looked out the peephole and saw two men running out the front door of the building. So we decided to hide out here in case they came back. That was a couple of hours ago."

"Well, I suggested we stop waiting here like sitting ducks and go to the cops," Sidney Allen said, his eyes flitting to my back door that led out onto the fire escape.

Leatrice shot him a look. "But I insisted we wait for the detective. I left him a message, but apparently he's out at a crime scene."

Another crime scene, I thought. So much for the holidays being about peace and goodwill toward men. Lately, Reese seemed to spend all his time at crime scenes.

I dropped my black Longchamp bag onto the floor next to the sofa and headed toward the kitchen, with Hermès close at my heels. "Do you think someone was trying to rob you?"

It seemed like a bad plan for burglars to pick the apartment on the first floor closest to the front door. Anyone could see what they were doing from the street, since the building's wooden front door was half glass. I peered inside the refrigerator and groaned when I realized there was nothing to drink but Reese's microbrews and one opened can of Diet Dr Pepper. I picked the opened can.

"I think someone saw my car last night and they're coming after me," Leatrice said, her head poking over the counter dividing my kitchen and living room.

Leatrice did have a distinctive car, but even if they spotted it near our building, they'd have no way to know which apartment was hers. "How could they track you down by your car?"

Hermès ran in circles around my feet and I patted his head. "Sorry, buddy. No more prosciutto."

He gave me a disgusted look and flounced out of the kitchen. It was scary how much the little Yorkie reminded me of Richard. I took a drink of the flat soda as I headed back to the living room.

"Easy," Leatrice said. "License plate records."

I sank onto the couch. "But those aren't public record, are they?"

Leatrice looked at me like I was a simpleton. "Cops can access them, along with anyone who can hack into their system."

Leatrice didn't need to remind me that she'd once used some friends she'd made on the dark web to hack into the DC police computers. I'm sure she didn't want Sidney Allen to know every sordid detail about her past, or have to explain why she was online friends with guys called Boots and Dagger Dan.

I took another sip of the syrupy sweet drink, making a mental note to go shopping soon. "So you think these guys somehow got into the records, used your license plate to get your address, and came here tonight to ...?"

"Intimidate me, scare me into silence, eliminate me," Leatrice said, listing the options off on her fingers as the color drained from her honeybun's face.

"It's not like you witnessed a crime," I said, thinking Leatrice's imagination and desire to see a conspiracy around every corner might be making her jump to conclusions.

"Maybe we did," Leatrice said. "Sure, we think we didn't see anything, but they don't know that. What if we caught them in the middle of a drug deal or a smuggling operation? Why else would a guy with a gun chase after us?"

I agreed with her that the guy chasing the car hadn't been normal behavior, but it seemed like a big leap to think that they'd tracked down Leatrice and were now after her. Although, knowing that Leatrice seemed to land in as many sticky situations as I did, I couldn't discount the possibility altogether. "Why don't I call Reese? He'll know what to do."

Leatrice sat down next to me and Hermès jumped up beside her, both tucking their feet up under themselves. Sidney Allen took the chair opposite, teetering on the edge as if he might need to leap to his feet at any moment.

"Thank you, Annabelle," he said. "Tell Mike we appreciate any help he can give."

Sidney Allen had unexpectedly bonded with my fiancé, and Reese had even been the best man in his wedding to Leatrice. I found it amazing that both Sidney Allen and Richard had a bromance going with Reese, and hoped there wouldn't be a brawl between the two divas one day.

I pulled out my phone and speed dialed my fiancé.

"Babe," he said when he answered, sounding out of breath. "I'm glad you called. Are you okay? Are you at home?"

"Yes, I'm at home. Why wouldn't I be okay?"

"I'm on the way to the building now. Don't leave our apartment."

"Okay." I sat up and put the empty soda can on the coffee table. "Now you're scaring me. What's going on?"

"I was just called to a crime scene in the alley behind our building."

CHAPTER 31

"**A**re those the two men you saw outside your apartment?" I asked Leatrice and Sidney Allen as we peered down the fire escape to the alley below.

Even though we were three stories up, I could tell that the men tied with their hands and feet behind their backs were broad-shouldered with dark hair and equally dark clothes. Several uniformed officers walked around the scene, and I saw my fiancé squatting next to the unconscious men. Apparently, the police had received an anonymous call that two criminals were tied up in the alley behind P Street. It appeared that they'd been knocked out as they were walking to the white paneled van that was parked off to the side.

Leatrice squinted and leaned over the metal railing. "It's hard to say, dearie. I really only saw their backs as they were running away, but it could be them. They look wide enough."

"It doesn't matter," I said, repeating what Reese had texted me. "These guys were already wanted by the police, so they'll be going to jail regardless."

"That makes me feel better," Leatrice said.

"What's on their heads?" Sidney Allen asked, taking a step back from the rail, his face pale.

"Santa hats." I thought I recognized one of the officers as the rookie

Kate and I had talked to at the station. I stepped back from the railing in case he looked up. I didn't want him to be reminded of our visit, especially since it didn't seem like he'd mentioned it to Reese.

"Isn't that nice they're getting into the spirit of things?" Leatrice smiled. "Not enough people dress for the season anymore."

Since Leatrice had a special outfit for every holiday, including the minor ones like Flag Day and Arbor Day, I'm sure she felt the rest of us were slackers.

"I'm pretty sure they didn't decide to wear those hats," I said, rubbing my hands over my arms to warm them. "Santa paraphernalia has been turning up at a lot of crime scenes lately, mostly on the criminals."

"Fascinating," Leatrice said, flipping up the hood of her footie pajamas.

Sidney Allen waved us toward the door. "Why don't we go inside? It's getting cold out here."

He was right. It was getting cold. I felt like cheering as I realized the temperature had dropped significantly since earlier in the evening. Maybe our winter wonderland wedding wouldn't feel so out of place after all.

We went back into my apartment, and I double-checked that the door was bolted. I'd installed heavy-duty locks on my back entrance after a break-in a couple of years ago. Even though the memory shouldn't have been a good one, it always reminded me of my fiancé, since the murder case connected to the break-in was the reason we'd met. It was also the first time I'd meddled in his case, or as I liked to think of it, the first time we'd worked together.

"How about some hot chocolate?" I asked, heading to the kitchen.

"You have that?" Leatrice asked, padding after me in her pajamaed feet that looked like bear claws.

I tried not to be offended by the surprised tone. "Of course I do. And some gourmet ginger cookies."

"Goodness." Leatrice rubbed her hands together. "I'm not used to fancy food at your apartment unless Richard is around." She paused at the doorway to the kitchen, her eyes wide. "He's not hiding in here, is he?"

LAURA DURHAM

"No. I do not have Richard stashed in the pantry." I didn't explain that I could offer them such a luxurious treat because I'd received both the Williams Sonoma hot chocolate and the cookies as a holiday gift from one of our favorite photographers.

One of the nicest parts of December, aside from the fact that we were usually less busy, was getting thoughtful gifts from the vendors we sent business to all year. I'd gotten everything from a Four Seasons bathrobe to spa gift certificates to designer purses. The purses were always from Richard because he lamented my dearth of designer bags. Receiving the gift box today had reminded me that Kate and I had yet to order the holiday gifts *we* sent to vendors. One more thing to add to my to-do list, I thought, before pushing that aside and reaching for the red cylindrical tin of hot chocolate.

"Who do you think did that?" Sidney Allen asked from the living room.

I poked my head over the dividing counter from the kitchen. Hermès was curled up in a brown-and-black ball on the couch, and Sidney Allen sat perched on the edge of my overstuffed chair, rocking himself back and forth and wringing his hands. He reminded me of Humpty Dumpty, and I hoped he wasn't about to take a great fall.

"I think your husband might need a little comforting," I whispered to Leatrice, who still lingered in the doorway.

She immediately hurried over to him and began rubbing his back. "I'm sure Reese will get to the bottom of it, whatever happened. He's such a smart young man."

Sidney Allen smiled and nodded. "That's true."

I pulled down three "Twelve Days of Christmas" mugs from an overhead cabinet--part of a set from the Willard Hotel last Christmas--and began scooping dark chocolate shavings into each one. "If you ask me, whoever tied up those guys is the hero in all this."

"Really?" Sidney Allen asked.

I checked my fridge for milk, then finding none, filled my tea kettle with water and put it on the stove. Hot chocolate with hot water wouldn't be so bad, I thought, adding milk to my mental shopping list.

"Sure," I said. "I'm willing to bet that the guys tied up in our alley

172

have a record or an outstanding arrest warrant or something. Everyone who's been tied up and turned in to the police dressed in Santa getup has turned out to be guilty as sin."

"So someone's cleaning up the city for Christmas?" he said, his voice sounding less shaky.

"Fern thinks that someone is Kris Kringle Jingle," Leatrice added.

I opened the round tin of Moravian Ginger Spice cookies and arranged a few on a plate, inhaling the sweet aroma of the thin cookies shaped like bells, snowmen, and stockings.

"What does Reese think?" Sidney Allen asked.

"You know him," I said, looking over the divider at my two elderly neighbors. "He doesn't want to say anything until he's positive."

"And he doesn't want to give Annabelle any more reason to get involved in his case," Leatrice said in a stage whisper.

I decided not to argue with her on that because I knew she was probably right. "Like I told Reese, I haven't been meddling this time. *We* seem to be stumbling into connections to Kris and all the Santa crimes."

I made a point not to mention talking to Stanley dressed as Santa. Not only would Leatrice read too much into it, nothing he'd said made sense. It was one of the main reasons I hadn't mentioned it to my fiancé. That, and he'd never believe Kate and I had run into the man by chance.

Leatrice flushed. "I suppose it was a Santa Claus who tipped me off to the stolen flowers in the dumpster, but how is Kris managing to do all these things?"

I decided it wouldn't hurt to tell Leatrice what I knew about the singing Santa. "Since he's lived on the streets for a while, he clearly knows how to get around without being seen. Plus, he served in Vietnam. Naval intelligence."

Leatrice gasped. "He's a veteran and he's homeless?"

"I'm afraid there are quite a few homeless vets in the city," I told her.

She shook her head. "I don't like that one bit."

"I don't think anyone does." I plucked the kettle off the burner as it started to whistle. "I had no idea he'd served until Fern told me."

"Well, we have to find him," Leatrice said, slapping the side of the chair and making both her fiancé and Hermès jump.

Stifling a laugh, I poured steaming hot water into the mugs and watched the chocolate shavings dissolve. "That's what we've been trying to do, but he's been pretty good at hiding so far."

"There must be a reason he's hiding," Sidney Allen said.

"Well, if he's the Santa vigilante, he's ticking off a bunch of pretty dangerous people." I carried two mugs out to the living room and handed one each to Leatrice and Sidney Allen. "I might be hiding too if I were him."

"Just think, sugar pie." Leatrice nudged Sidney Allen. "We've got our own crime-fighting Santa."

I returned to the kitchen for my mug and the cookies, walking back to the living room and sinking onto the couch next to Hermès, who gave me a disdainful look out of one eye before rearranging himself and going back to sleep. Taking a sip of the rich chocolate, I thought how much better it would be with milk. And maybe whipped cream on the top.

"You don't think he takes requests, do you?" Leatrice asked, her eyes sparkling over the rim of her mug. "I'm still convinced the guy in 2B is a sleeper agent for some foreign government."

I thought about Brianna slashing Kate's tires and stealing our flower order. "If he does, get in line."

CHAPTER 32

"Who knew you'd have a more exciting night than me?" Kate said the next day as we stood side by side in the Four Seasons ballroom and watched as large icicle lights were hung from the ceiling.

"It might be a first." I turned to take in the room, feeling pleased by the transformation of the room from hotel chic to winter wonderland.

The walls had been draped from floor to ceiling in white gossamer fabric with blue twinkle lights strung behind the layers of fabric. The dance floor was transparent and blinked with blue pinprick lights every time someone stepped on it. Clusters of birch branches ringed the room and were uplit so shadows of the branches crisscrossed the ceiling. Long, rectangular tables were draped in a sparkly white linen, and tall arrangements of branches cuffed with white hydrangea-- successfully rehydrated by Buster and Mack--ran the length of each table. Silver base plates sat at each place, and round mirrored menus fit perfectly in the center, the words written in swirling white calligra- phy. The ladder-backed chairs were clear, and large snowflake tags hung off each one with a guest's name written in silver ink—our creative alternative to a place card.

"So the bad guys got hauled off to jail, and Kris is still on the loose?" Kate asked, walking over and straightening a white linen napkin on the nearest table. "Along with Santa Stanley?"

"We don't know that Kris did it," I said. "We just know that the guys were wearing Santa hats."

"Come on." Kate narrowed her eyes at me. "Who else would be doing this? Who else is obsessed with Santa Claus?"

"Aside from millions of children? Besides, these deliveries or reports of criminals in Santa gear started before Kris disappeared."

"But not long before, and maybe that's why he staged his own murder and went into hiding." Kate shifted from one ridiculously high heel to the other. "Of course, it could be Stanley. We saw him dressed as Santa and he seemed pretty wired. I wouldn't put vigilante past him."

"I don't know why either man doesn't come out of hiding now. It's not like they'd be in trouble for helping the police lock up a bunch of bad guys."

"Maybe Kris can't," Kate said with a shrug. "Maybe he feels like he's still in danger. I doubt he's rounded up all the criminals in town, and some of the big guys might be a little upset that their colleagues have been arrested. Stanley seemed to think it wasn't safe."

"Stanley said a lot of strange stuff," I reminded her.

"Is this spacing good?" Our lighting guy, John, called down from the top of a tall ladder.

I gave him a thumbs-up. "Perfect. These will be on a dimmer, right?"

He nodded and went back to hanging the icicle lights.

"At least the weather finally fits our theme," I said, waving for Kate to follow me out of the ballroom. "We won't have to crank up the AC to make people think it's winter."

Kate rubbed her hands together. "Finally my boots won't look ridiculous."

"It wasn't so much the boots that looked ridiculous. It was that they were paired with shorts. Really short shorts."

"Because it was really hot. If I'd worn boots and pants, I'd have been baking." She shook her head at me. "Don't blame me for the heat wave."

We walked into the foyer and across to the Dumbarton room, where Buster and Mack were setting up cocktail hour. Instead of white decor with touches of blue, this room was all ice blue with accents of white. The linens on the scattered high-top tables were a frosty blue, and the round bar in the center of the room was white acrylic lit from inside with blue LEDs. A curtain of white lights hung from the ceiling, filling it from end to end.

I spotted Mack installing a massive arrangement of white branches in the middle of the bar, his plus-sized leather pants and jacket a sharp contrast to the pale colors around him.

He waved at us. "What do you think?"

"The bride will love it," Kate called back.

Mack grinned then dropped a branch. "Elf on the shelf!" He ducked behind the bar to retrieve it, mumbling more sanitized holiday curses.

Buster walked up behind us, holding a pair of small square bowls jammed with fluffy white hydrangea. "Thanks to you. I don't know what we would have done without our flowers."

"All in a day's work." I patted his thick arm.

"One of our days, at least," Kate said. "Probably not your normal wedding planner's day."

I tried not to take offense since she was right. I liked to think Kate and I were a few levels above average, and our crew was definitely not your typical wedding planning team.

Buster laughed. "I delivered the bouquets. The bride loved them."

"How's she doing?" Kate asked. "When we left her to check on the ballroom, breakfast for her and the bridesmaids had just arrived."

As planned, Kate and I had arrived when hair and makeup had started, checking in on a tired bride still bubbling about the ski lodge rehearsal dinner the night before. Richard's food had been a huge success, as had his "to go" s'mores favors tied with miniature ski poles. The bridesmaids were still munching on the chocolate bars this morning, while they walked around the spacious suite in powder blue bathrobes with their names embroidered on the back. As we'd ducked out to check on setup, a waiter had been wheeling in a cart filled with bagels, muffins, and plates of sliced fruit.

Buster bit the corner of his bottom lip. "She seemed happy. Fern was making all the orange juice into mimosas."

I sighed. "How long until the mimosas become straight glasses of champagne?"

"And how long after that until Fern starts teasing everyone's hair too high?" Kate asked.

Knowing Fern when the bubbly and his creative juices got flowing, he could decide to make all the bridesmaids' hair resemble Christmas trees complete with blinking lights.

"We'd better get up there," I said. "You know how peeved he gets when we make him redo hair."

"Go." Buster shooed us away. "We've got everything under control down here."

We thanked him, waved to Mack, and headed out of the room. I paused at the large round table at the bottom of the stairs and touched a hand to the fake snow that covered it. Tucked into the faux snow-drift was a guest book and family photos in silver frames.

"You don't seem stressed about Brianna anymore," I said to Kate. "All I'm picking up is normal wedding day stress."

"Didn't I tell you?" She twisted to face me. "I texted one of Brianna's assistants. The one who comes to the assistant happy hours. She told me they don't have cameras in the office."

"And you waited all this time to tell me?" I shook my head. "Did the assistant think your question was strange?"

"I doubt it. I told her we were considering a security camera system and asked if they had one she could recommend."

I nodded at her. "Not bad."

Kate kept walking and glanced back over her shoulder, winking at me. "Does this mean I can get out of doing escort cards?"

"Nice try." I looked at the towering frosted Christmas tree positioned next to the table. "Don't you mean escort ornaments? And we have to wait until Buster and Mack add the silver ribbon garland to the tree first."

Instead of traditional cards to let guests know at which table they were seated, we'd come up with the idea of glass Christmas ornaments with names written on them in shiny silver calligraphy. It had seemed like a fun idea when we'd thought of it, but now we were tasked with hanging over a hundred breakable balls on a tree in some semblance of alphabetical order.

Kate groaned. "Setting them out might be my least favorite part of the wedding day. After lining up the bridal party for the processional."

"What about loading people onto shuttle buses?"

She snapped her fingers. "I almost forgot how much I loathe that. That's still number three after the processional and place cards. Thank you for reminding me, Annabelle."

I grinned at her as I joined her at the base of the stairs. "Anytime."

Kate's mouth dropped open, and she grabbed my arm. "Did you just see that?"

"See what?" I followed her gaze out the glass walls to the canal terrace.

"Santa." She touched a hand to the side of her head. "I could have sworn I just saw Santa Claus run by."

CHAPTER 33

"**D**oesn't the hotel have a Santa?" I asked as we reached the hotel's lobby, which was filled with at least a dozen towering Christmas trees, each one uniquely decorated. The hotel went all out for the holiday, so a roaming Santa didn't seem out of the realm of possibility.

"Only for special parties." Kate paused as a group of tourists passed us, so distracted by the ornately decorated trees that they almost ran into us. "And why would Santa be running around the outside of the hotel?"

We'd rushed to the glass walls that overlooked the C&O Canal, but there had been no sign of a Santa. We'd even ducked outside and looked up and down the canal. Nothing.

"Is it possible you're imagining Santa since so many have been popping up?" I asked, inhaling the heady scent of Christmas tree and leading the way through the busy lobby toward the elevator bank.

"Like PTSD?" she said. "Post Traumatic Santa Disorder?"

I gave her a withering look. "Post Traumatic *Stress* Disorder is a real thing. This is not."

As we passed a pair of upholstered chairs tucked against one wall, a deep throat clearing made me turn my head. "Daniel? Is that you?"

My fiancé's older brother stood. He had the same dark hair as

Reese, although it was flecked with gray at the temples, and was only a fraction taller. Both men were handsome enough to turn heads, and I saw a woman near us do a quick double take.

"What a coincidence," I said, glancing around. "Are you working?"

Daniel Reese had been a DC cop before leaving to open his own private security firm. He now worked with an elite clientele, so it was easy to imagine his client would be staying at The Four Seasons.

Daniel looked at Kate. "You could say that."

"He's our bodyguard," Kate said, sidling up next to him. "I thought with everything going on with Brianna, we could use some extra muscle."

Even though it was widely known that Kate had a special talent for determining if people were dating with a single glance, it didn't take a relationship guru to know that something more was going on. Was this the older man she'd been talking about? I never would have called him "older," but I suppose he was older than Kate by about a decade. I decided to leave that topic for later.

"You hired security for our wedding without mentioning it to me?"

She smiled up at Daniel. "I wouldn't say hired."

"I'm doing this pro bono," Daniel said, pushing up the sleeves of his black blazer.

"And it's not for the wedding as much as it's for us," Kate said. "You said yourself that Brianna's obsession with us was turning violent. She knows we have a wedding here today. She might know we got the flowers back. She could know we snuck into her place."

"We don't know that for sure."

She flapped a hand in the air. "The long and short of it is that we need someone watching our backs."

She might have a point. Things with Brianna had gotten ugly, despite my initial efforts to make peace. If the planner really was behind the damage to Kate's car and the pilfering of our flowers, she was out of control. I wouldn't put it past her to show up and try to sabotage our wedding or even hurt one of us.

"Fine," I said. "You might be right."

Kate looped her arm through Daniel's. "I sent him a photo of

Brianna, so he can keep an eye out for her while we focus on the wedding."

"I'll be discreet," he said.

In his black suit, I knew he'd look just like a wedding guest. A handsome, muscular wedding guest. Our bigger problem might be keeping the bridesmaids off him once they'd had a few drinks.

"Thanks." Since Daniel and I would be family one day, I wasn't sure if I should hug him or what, so I squeezed his arm. I still hadn't gotten used to the idea that I would have a brother-in-law. I'd barely adjusted to the concept of a fiancé.

We left him in the lobby while we proceeded to the bride's suite. As we rode the elevator up, I tapped the toe of my black flat.

"So you and Daniel?"

Kate swung her head to me, her cheeks splotched with pink. "Maybe. Why? Do you think he's too old for me?"

I held up both palms as the elevator doors pinged open. "Not at all. I think he's great. I'm marrying the slightly younger version, remember?"

She laughed nervously. "Right. Of course. He's a lot more laid-back when he's not working, you know."

"You don't need to convince me. As long as you're not just playing around with him. I doubt he's the kind of guy who's casual about anything."

"That's the weird thing." She nibbled the edge of her thumbnail as we walked down the hallway toward the bride's suite. "I've lost my urge to date around since I started seeing him."

I fought the urge to check if she had a fever. "That's a good thing. It shows you may be ready to stick with one guy and maybe settle down in the near future."

She didn't say anything else, and a few seconds later, we'd reached the propped-open door to the bridal suite. A haze of hairspray had drifted out into the hall, making me cough as we approached. I could hear the din of hip-hop music along with lots of female voices and one very distinct male voice.

"All right, tramps," he called out over the music. "Who's next to get bedazzled?"

I glanced at Kate. "That's not a good sign."

Pushing the door open, I spotted a blond bridesmaid dancing by in her monogrammed robe. As she turned around, I clutched Kate's arm for support. "Is that...?"

"A braid around the back of her head that looks like a Christmas wreath?" Kate patted my hand. "Sure is."

Fern had woven green ribbon through the circular braid and tied a red bow at the bottom. It would have been ideal for a flower girl, but looked silly on a grown woman. I suspected that everyone in the room had imbibed too much champagne to realize that a wreath on the back of their heads was not a style that would age well in photos. A French twist? Classic. A wreath made of hair? Not so much.

I led the way through the room, dodging a conga line of brides-maids and passing the picked-over breakfast cart along with multiple bottles of champagne on end tables, coffee tables, and ice buckets. One look at the dancing bridesmaids told me they were all empty.

I saw Fern set up by the windows with the bride sitting in front of him on a stool. He wore a red velvet suit with white piping and his favorite black Ferragamo belt.

"Maybe this is who I mistook for Santa," Kate said.

"You're back." Fern beamed when he saw us, waving with the hand holding a champagne flute. "What do you think of the bridesmaids?"

"I think it isn't what we discussed," I said through a plastered on smile so the bride wouldn't think I was upset. I gave her a quick hug and told her she looked stunning.

"Do you mind if I take a quick bathroom break?" she asked, slipping off the stool.

"Take your time, sweetie," Fern said, smiling as she hurried off, then leaning in to me. "I'm not surprised she has to go again. That girl's been drinking like a fish all morning."

"That would explain why she's fine with the hair wreaths," Kate muttered.

I cut my eyes to a passing bridesmaid, then narrowed my eyes at Fern. "Explain."

Fern fluttered a hand at me. "I got a burst of creative inspiration. Besides, it's a Christmas wedding."

"Actually, it's a winter wonderland wedding. Everything is blue and white."

He frowned then shrugged. "Well, it's almost Christmas. It will look marvelously festive at the church. I can change up their hair for the reception. Maybe put crystals in instead."

"Don't even think about doing anything but the classic updo you did at the bride's hair trial."

He let out a deeply wounded sigh. "You're no fun when it comes to themes, sweetie. What about some sprigs of holly? No? Fine, but those wreaths make a statement."

I folded my arms over my chest. "Yes, and it's 'Don't drink and do hair.'"

"Hurtful," Fern said, touching a hand to his chest, his enormous topaz ring flashing at me.

"Where's Carl?" I asked, scanning the room for our makeup artist.

"He had to run out to grab more mascara." Fern made a tsk-ing noise in the back of his throat. "He ran out of waterproof."

You couldn't put a bride in regular mascara unless you wanted her to look like a crying banshee.

"Love the suit," Kate said, waving at Fern's outfit. "It fits you better than the Santa suit."

"It's hard to get a slim fit Santa costume," Fern said, pulling a brush through the bride's hair and taking a drink of champagne. "Besides, my Santa costume disappeared. Didn't I tell you?"

"Disappeared?" I asked. "Do you mean it was stolen?"

Fern twitched one shoulder up and down. "I left it in my storage room, and I left the key over the doorsill for Kris, so I assume he's borrowing it."

"Or a drug kingpin is wearing it bound and gagged," Kate muttered.

"You probably should start locking your back door," I told Fern. "Just in case it isn't Kris."

"But then I never would have gotten this note from him," Fern said, producing a crumpled piece of paper from his impossibly snug pants pocket.

I took the paper and unfolded it, reading the note written by Fern at the top in which he asked Kris if he'd been the Santa at the dumpster. Below Fern's swirling handwriting was a hastily scrawled response.

Not me. Look for 4263.

"What's 4263?" Kate asked, leaning across me as she read the note.

Fern shrugged. "No idea. An address?"

I stared at the paper, the ink smudged. "But what street? This could be anywhere."

"And those numbers don't exist in Georgetown addresses," Fern reminded me. "Not Georgetown proper, at least. An address with 4263 would be much higher up Wisconsin or deeper into downtown."

I let out a breath, frustrated that the tip from our renegade Santa was so vague.

"Why be so cagey?" Kate asked. "Why not just tell us?"

I folded the paper and tucked it into my pocket. "Maybe he doesn't trust us."

Kate opened her arms wide. "Then why say anything at all? He clearly wants us to find something at 4263 or he wouldn't have mentioned it."

"But he felt he couldn't say it directly." I shook my head, more confused than ever.

I felt my phone buzz in my pocket and I pulled it out, turning to Kate before answering. "Keep an eye on the hair while I take this."

She stepped closer to Fern, taking the glass of champagne from his hand and stealing a sip.

I pressed the talk button as I walked toward the door, expecting it to be one of my wedding vendors checking in. "Annabelle Archer speaking."

"Babe, it's me," Reese said.

"Oh, hey." I felt a rush hearing his voice. "Guess who I just saw in the lobby of The Four Seasons."

He sighed deeply. "That's what I was calling to tell you. I told her not to bother you."

"Her?" I stepped out into the hallway, pulling the door almost closed to block out the sound of Beyoncé singing about all the single ladies.

"As I was leaving for work, Leatrice was heading out in her Santa suit to sing carols around Georgetown and insisted she was going to surprise you at the Four Seasons."

"That explains the Santa Kate saw running around outside the hotel," I said, shaking my head. "I have *got* to stop telling her where I'm working. I didn't know you were working today."

"Got called in." He sighed. "I just walked into the precinct."

"You might be able to help with this." I walked a few steps down the carpeted hallway, the sound of bridesmaids' laughter becoming fainter. "Fern got a note--most likely from Kris--telling him to look for 4263. Does that ring any bells? Is it the location of someplace notable in the criminal underworld?"

He chuckled. "4263? The criminal underworld? Not that I know of. I can do a search for addresses and see what I come up with."

"Thanks. I don't know why he's sending us code. Why not just tell us?"

"He's former military," Reese reminded me. "And it sounds like he's scared. Maybe he thought the note would be seen by the wrong person and get him into deeper trouble."

"Who's Fern going to show aside from us? The president of the Junior League?"

Another laugh from Reese. "Did you say Kate saw a Santa running around the Four Seasons? When was this?"

"About twenty minutes ago."

"I hate to break it to you, but that couldn't have been Leatrice. She only left our building twenty minutes ago."

I rubbed a hand across my forehead. "So you're telling me I have to deal with multiple Santas, a cryptic code that makes no sense, and a huge wedding?"

Reese chuckled. "'Tis the season, babe."

CHAPTER 34

"So I wasn't seeing things?" Kate asked as we stepped off the elevator at the lobby level.

We were greeted by piped-in holiday music and the low hum of visitors admiring the Christmas trees. I knew that in an hour or two the sun would set and the hotel's restaurant would also get busy. Hotels in December were always bustling--another reason we usually avoided holiday weddings.

"I'm not saying that," I said. "Just that between Fern's missing Santa suit, Leatrice in a Santa suit, and the fact that it's almost Christmas, there's a good chance we might see more than one Santa today."

I glanced at the empty upholstered chair where we'd left Daniel. "Where do you think he ran off to?"

"He's probably doing a perimeter sweep."

I raised an eyebrow at her. "Look who knows the security team lingo."

She gave a nervous laugh. "I've heard him talking to his guys a few times. You pick it up."

I understood that. After hearing Reese talk to Hobbes on the phone, I felt like I was learning the various codes they used to short-hand their conversations. "Let's forget about Leatrice and the fact that we have a private security guard and just focus on the wedding. We still need to hang those escort ornaments."

"No time like a present," Kate said.

"*The* present," I said under my breath, knowing she didn't care.

She twitched one shoulder up and down. "My version is more Christmassy."

As we crossed the lobby toward the stairs going down, I glanced over and saw a Santa coming through the glass front doors of the hotel. I tugged Kate along behind me. "Move it. I think I see Leatrice."

"You know she'll track us down eventually," Kate said as we hurried down the stairs. "You're just delaying the inevitable."

"If she can get past the hotel security," I said. "Short Santa with lots of makeup should send up some red flags."

We reached the ballroom level, and I saw that Buster and Mack had added the silver ribbon garland to our escort card tree. Behind the tree, a bright red leg and shiny black boot disappeared into the meeting room we'd set aside as the bride and groom's quiet space for when they arrived at the hotel after the ceremony and before they joined cocktail hour.

"Who was that?" I asked, fighting the urge to rub my eyes.

"Who was who?"

"Okay, I could have sworn I just saw the leg of a Santa go into the bride and groom's holding room."

"It couldn't be Leatrice. We just saw her upstairs." Kate clutched my arm. "We're being stalked by Santas. It's like a terrifying holiday horror movie."

I rushed over and peeked inside the room. Nothing. Of course the Santa could have gone out the back of the room that led to the hotel kitchens and prep area, but why would a Santa be sneaking around the bowels of a hotel?

"We're not being stalked by Santas," I said, joining Kate in the foyer again. "The hotel probably has one appearing in the restaurant or a private party or something. You know corporate holiday parties love their Santas."

"You know who would know?" Kate snapped her fingers. "Sidney Allen. Doesn't he supply most of the Santas around DC?"

"You're a genius." I pulled out my phone and searched up the entertainment diva's number, calling him and waiting until he picked up. " Hi, Sidney Allen. It's Annabelle."

"Hi, Annabelle." He sounded surprised to hear from me, and I could hear the worry in his voice. "We aren't working together today, are we?"

"No. Not today. I have a quick question for you."

"Okay. Hold on one second. Dickens carolers, I need you on the balcony pronto." He was clearly talking into the headset he always wore when coordinating entertainment at events. "Waifs, I need you to emote more. I need more waif from you. Okay, Annabelle, I'm back; what can I do for you?"

"Do you have any Santas at the Four Seasons today?"

"Today?" He went quiet for a moment. "Nope. We're at the Fairmont, the Park Hyatt, and the Mayflower. We're not at the Four Seasons again until a holiday party on Wednesday."

"Thanks. Sorry to bother you."

"Don't mention it," he said, then sucked in a sharp breath. "Carolers from the eighteenth century did not wear digital watches, Kenneth. Did you miss my email on historical accuracy? I have to run, Annabelle." And with that, he clicked off.

"So?" Kate asked.

"He doesn't have any Santas here, and I feel really sorry for Kenneth." I let out a breath. "We still have a wedding to run and ornaments to hang. Let's try to forget about the Santa sightings and focus on that."

"Agreed." Kate led the way to the meeting room next door that we were using to store all of our supplies and details for the wedding. "Our wedding is the one thing that's been smooth sailing."

When we walked in, Mack stood at the long table that held the drinks and a silver punch bowl filled with ice. Later in the evening, it would hold a buffet of sandwiches, pasta salad, chips, and cookies for all the vendors. For now, it was empty save the assortment of miniature bottles of sodas and waters.

Mack looked up from pouring himself a Sprite. "There you are. Did you see the tree?"

"It looks great," I said as Kate joined him at the table, and I headed for the stacks of boxes along one wall. "Now all we have to do is hang these in alphabetical order without breaking any."

"You know guests are going to take forever trying to find their names, right?" Kate asked, twisting the top off a Diet Coke.

"That's why you'll be standing there to help them."

She rolled her eyes. "Why me?"

"Would you rather be in charge of wrangling the bridal party into order for the introductions?"

She cringed. "Never mind. I'll take tree duty."

I knelt down and read the sides of the cardboard boxes, searching for the box we'd labeled "A-F." I stood up and turned around. "Did we bring all the boxes from my apartment?"

"Of course. We read off the letters as we loaded them into your CRV."

"That's what I thought." I counted the boxes again. "And we definitely unloaded everything from my car?"

"You know we did." Kate walked over to join me. "What's going on?"

"The 'A-F' box isn't here."

"Impossible." Kate bent over and walked down the row of boxes, reading the side of each one. She glanced over her shoulder at Mack. "You guys didn't take it by any chance?"

Mack shook his head. "This is the first I've been in here all day."

My pulse quickened and I tried not to panic. This wasn't a situation where we could fix it with back-up escort cards. We didn't have twenty-five spare ornaments or the time to paint names on them.

"Brianna," Kate said like she was uttering a curse.

So much for our wedding setup going smoothly.

CHAPTER 35

A s soon as she said it, I knew she was right. Who else would have any use for Christmas ornaments with other people's names on them? Only someone who wanted to sabotage our wedding, and Brianna knew we had a wedding at the Four Seasons today. She'd already tried to sabotage it once by stealing the flowers, and now she'd stolen some of our escort cards.

"She's Santa," Kate said.

"What?" Mack stared at her.

I nodded. "You're right. The person who stole the flower order was dressed like Santa. What better way to move around in December without people recognizing you than a Santa suit?"

Kate pointed to the doorway that led into the back of the hotel. "And she's moving around through the back of the house."

"The loading dock," I said. "I'll bet she's heading for the loading dock."

Mack shook his head. "Our trucks are blocking the way out. We thought it was her who tried to steal candy from your Valentine's wedding last year and had to abandon it because she couldn't get out of the loading dock. I don't think she'll make that mistake again."

"If it was me, I'd walk right out the front door," Kate said. "Who's going to stop Santa?"

"I'll head upstairs," I said, waving to Kate. "Can you text Daniel and tell him to be on the lookout for a Santa with a box?"

"On it," Kate said, her fingers already tapping away on her phone.

"I'll go tell Buster," Mack said, walking out of the room with me. "He'd love an excuse to chase down Brianna."

I took the stairs to the lobby two at a time, grateful I wore sensible flats on wedding days and grateful Kate wasn't running behind me this time, trying to keep up in her very insensible heels. When I reached the lobby, I swung my head from side to side. The place was brimming with people, but I didn't see a Santa. Not even Leatrice dressed as Santa. I pushed through the tourists ooh-ing and aah-ing over the decor until I'd reached the glass doors.

"Annabelle, dear!"

I spun to see Leatrice sitting on a cream-colored couch in the lobby's sitting area. As expected, she had on a Santa suit--sans the beard--and a full face of makeup. A uniformed police officer stood next to her looking less than pleased.

"Is everything okay?" As much as I wanted to catch Brianna, I didn't want Leatrice to get arrested, although I couldn't imagine what the octogenarian had done.

"Fine and dandy," she said, straightening her red-and-white hat.

"You know this Santa?" the officer asked. "We got a call from hotel security about some unauthorized Santas wandering around the hotel."

"I know her," I said. "She's my neighbor and she's harmless, if a little excited about the holidays. You can check with Detective Mike Reese. He'll vouch for her, as well."

The cop's eyebrows went up. "Thanks." The corners of his mouth curved up. "So when she threatened to give her detective friend my badge number, she wasn't kidding?"

I gave Leatrice a stern look, but she merely shrugged, holding up a slip of paper with numbers written on it along with a name.

"I'm sorry, officer." I scanned the lobby again. "Neither of you have seen another Santa come through here by any chance?"

Leatrice's garishly coral lips curled up into a wide smile. "Actually, I did. Just a minute ago."

"Where did she go?"

"She?" Leatrice blinked rapidly. "There's another lady Santa in Georgetown?"

"It's not a real Santa. It's Brianna, dressed as Santa, trying to sabotage our wedding."

Leatrice frowned. "That's not very Christmassy of her." She pointed at the glass doors. "She walked right out the front of the hotel."

"Thanks." I waved at her as I ran out of the hotel. Brianna didn't live here, and her office was all the way at the end of M Street, so I doubted she was walking all the way there carrying a big box. She had to have a getaway vehicle.

It was already dusk outside, and I squinted as I looked around. The hotel valets were busy running back and forth as cars swung into the circular drive that fronted the hotel, but I didn't see a Santa in any of the cars. I glanced back through the glass doors to the police officer, and I almost gasped out loud.

4263

It couldn't be, I thought, as I punched in Reese's number on my phone. It went to voicemail.

"Elf me!" I said loudly, making a valet give me a curious look. I'd gotten so used to Buster and Mack's alternative curses, I'd forgotten how to swear properly. I left a message explaining my theory and clicked off.

I still needed to find Brianna and our missing ornaments, plus I had no idea of knowing if my wild hunch was right. Hurrying to the left of the hotel, toward Twenty-ninth Street and the nearest street parking, a noise drew my attention to the Four Seasons courtyard tucked back between two buildings.

"Don't move, Kris." The voice wasn't loud, but it was forceful, and I knew I'd heard it before.

I followed the sound--walking quietly on my toes--until I'd reached the paved area scattered with outdoor seating and a round raised flower bed that now held only greenery. Since the temperature had dropped, no one was outside. No one but a Santa and a cop with his gun drawn.

A cop that I could see in the landscape uplighting had the badge number 4263. I'd been right about the number being a policeman's badge. The cop mentioning Leatrice wanting to take his badge number had made me realize the connection, but I hadn't been sure who the badge would belong to. Until now.

I didn't make a sound as I watched Officer Rogers, and the Santa I was sure was Brianna, facing away from him and holding a cardboard box in her arms.

It all made sense. Officer Rogers had been the one to suggest that Stanley had killed Kris, which sent us off on a tangent. He'd also been at Fern's break-in, so he probably suspected that Kris wasn't dead, and when the blood results came back, he knew Kris was alive. If he had a reason to want the singing Santa dead, he'd probably been trying to track him down—and Stanley, as well—for days. It explained why Stanley was so nervous and why he didn't trust us when Kate mentioned that I was engaged to a cop. He had no way of knowing if my cop was the bad one or not.

I swallowed hard as I watched the officer steady his aim at Brianna. As much as I despised her, I couldn't let her get shot.

"That's not Kris." A second voice came from beneath one of the trees in the corner, and I had to stop myself from gasping as a second Santa emerged from the shadows of the branches. It was Kris Kringle Jingle and, from what I could tell in the eerie uplighting, he looked completely unscathed.

Rogers swung his gun to Kris. "I knew you weren't dead. Just like I knew Stanley planted your suit with the fake blood. Where is he, by the way?"

"Safe and out of your reach," Kris said. "Just like Jeannie and the others."

"How did you know?" Rogers asked.

Kris shrugged. "I didn't at first, then I realized why you seemed so familiar when you'd taken the Georgetown beat. You used to be in tight with the guys running drugs and stolen goods through my neighborhood. I'd seen you with them before, then I saw you with them the other night when they were packing up their trucks. Only you didn't stop them."

Brianna hadn't taken a step, but I saw her twist her head around.

"I thought I saw you running off that night," Rogers said, raising his gun higher. "I was just curious."

My heart pounded. Was he going to shoot Kris right here outside the Four Seasons? I opened my mouth to yell for help when the pop of a gun made my knees buckle. Brianna screamed and dropped the box, taking off through the courtyard toward the canal.

My eyes didn't leave Kris, who still stood, but I saw Rogers fly forward, the momentum causing him to spin and land on his back. Daniel rushed forward, his gun still drawn, and kicked Roger's gun out of the way.

"You shot him?" I managed to say, my voice barely a croak.

"In the shoulder, so he wouldn't shoot Santa here," Daniel said, glancing at me. "You okay?"

I nodded, even though I felt dizzy. Staggering to the raised flower bed, I sat on the brick border. Kris sat next to me while Daniel cuffed Rogers, who screamed as his arms were wrenched behind his back.

"So have you been behind all the criminals being nabbed and dressed up in Santa paraphernalia?" I asked him.

"Not just me." He tugged his white beard down so I could see his mouth. "All of my friends. When you live on the streets, you see everything that goes on. We didn't like that crime was on the rise, so we decided to take care of it our way."

"We saw Stanley last night. I assume he's been part of it?"

Kris rubbed a hand over his red belly. "Aside from helping me stage my own death, he's been helping me take out the bad guys. Stanley was special forces, so he's been a big help."

My stomach tightened. Another homeless vet. "Who tipped us off about the flowers in the dumpster? Was that you or Stanley?"

He shook his head, but grinned. "Jeannie, but it was me who took care of the guys who went into your building looking for your friend."

"I should have known when those goons were able to track Leatrice down so fast. She even said it. Only law enforcement or hackers have such fast access to license plate information. And those guys didn't look like hackers." My phone buzzed in my pocket, and I answered it when I saw Kate's name on the screen.

"Where are you, Annabelle?"

"In the courtyard with Kris Kringle Jingle." I patted the singing Santa on the leg. "It's all over."

"For you maybe," Kate said. "Buster and Mack just had to pull two brawling Santas apart down here. Leatrice had Brianna pinned down and was snapping her beard over and over."

"I'm sorry I missed that."

"No sign of the ornaments, though."

"I've got the box up here." I eyed the cardboard container Brianna had dropped and said a little prayer that they weren't all shattered. "And she definitely took it. I saw her with it in her hands before she ran off."

"Good. I, for one, look forward to pressing charges. I already called your man, so the cops should be here soon."

"I left him a message telling him what the clue meant." My heart leapt at the thought of seeing Reese. Even though I knew he wouldn't be thrilled to find me in the middle of another crime scene, there was no one I'd rather be comforted by. "And yours is up here cuffing Officer Rogers."

"Come again?"

"I'll tell you everything later," I told her, clicking off as I spotted Reese's car screech to a stop in the valet line, the portable police light flashing on top.

Kris stiffened next to me. "I guess I have some explaining to do."

"Don't worry," I said. "It's my fiancé. He's one of the good guys, like you." I stood up then turned back to him. "How would you and your Santa posse like to come to a party tomorrow?"

CHAPTER 36

"I'm not sure this screams engagement party," Fern said as he stood behind me the next afternoon pulling out the ponytail he'd been horrified to find me wearing when he'd arrived. "There's no diamond ring decor or giant love balloons."

I surveyed my apartment and stifled a yawn. "It's a holiday-themed engagement party. Heavy on the holidays."

"Heavy on the last minute," Richard grumbled as he passed us with a platter of hors d'ouevres to place on the dining room table turned food station.

"Too last minute to warn me that I wouldn't recognize the place when I came home last night?" Reese asked, coming down the hall in jeans and a snug cream sweater topped with a brown herringbone jacket.

Fern drew in his breath. "Merry Christmas to me." He dropped his voice and leaned close to my ear. "He looks good enough to dip in chocolate."

"I also styled your fiancé," Richard said. "The sweater and blazer are my Christmas gifts to him."

Richard liked to give gifts that he knew people would never give themselves. For me, that meant designer handbags he knew I'd never splurge on and because, as he'd once explained to me, "It hurts my eyes to see pleather." For Reese, that clearly meant clothes a DC detective probably couldn't afford. I didn't need to touch the blazer to know it had cashmere in the blend or look at the labels to know they were European.

"I think it's a gift for all of us," Fern said, making an approving noise in the back of his throat.

With his dark wavy hair brushed back and one curl falling over his forehead, Reese did look pretty hot. My pulse fluttered as he locked his hazel eyes on me. "You look great, babe."

Fern let out a breathy sigh, and I caught myself blushing. "Thanks."

I'd found a red plaid swirl skirt in the back of my closet and paired it with an ivory sweater with a deep cowl neckline and black boots. It might not be as designer as my fiancé's new outfit, but it was pretty festive.

Richard darted his gaze over me quickly. "Not bad, darling." He tucked one side of my sweater into the top of my skirt. "A little French tuck should do the trick. There. Now it works."

"Speaking of styling," I said, "any word on when our photo shoot will be in *DC Life Magazine*?"

"Actually, they've bumped it up to the January issue, which will be fabulous for business." Richard touched a hand to my sleeve. "All those newly engaged holiday brides will just be reaching the preliminary panic stage of planning when it hits the stands."

"Sounds fun," Reese said, winking at me.

A beeping sounded from the kitchen, and Richard hurried off muttering something about his pimento cheese puffs and last-minute parties.

While the rest of us had been running the wedding at the Four Seasons--or giving statements to the police about the proliferation of Santas running around at the wedding--Richard had been tasked by Kate to get my apartment ready for today's party. Considering how little focus we'd all had to give the event, I thought he'd done an admirable job. I didn't even mind the fact that he'd repurposed items from past holiday parties.

I recognized the gold sparkly table runner from a recent house party he'd splashed all over his Instagram feed and suspected the matte gold antlers tucked into the glittering garland and ornaments filling the runner were from Friday night's rehearsal dinner (and courtesy of a coat of spray paint). White feathers tucked around the antlers were from an art deco wedding we'd had over the summer, and the gold striped paper straws on the counter between the kitchen and living room that now served as the bar were leftover from a client's baby shower. Shiny gold balls filled glass bowls and tall cylinders and were placed on nearly every available surface.

My usual piles of wedding magazines and Reese's *Sports Illustrateds* had been whisked away and replaced with decorative stacks of books covered in gold paper. I knew the book's contents were irrelevant as they were only there for visual impact, and I suspected they had been snagged from my bookshelf, as I noticed a few gaps in the rows. Even my usual throw pillows had been switched out for metallic gold versions, several with trendy phrases like "Baby It's Cold Outside" and "Let It Snow." The only element untouched was the tall Christmas tree in the corner, which had already been decorated by Richard in tip-to-trunk metallic.

"Shouldn't Kate be here by now?" Fern asked, spraying my hair with a travel-sized hairspray that he must have secreted away in his winter white suit, although I couldn't imagine how, since it fit him like a glove.

"I'm sure she's on her way. It was a long night for us. After all the drama with Brianna and Kris Kringle, we still had to run the wedding."

"You don't have to tell me." Fern unleashed a cloud of spray over my head. "I had to change out all the bridesmaids' hair after the ceremony, remember?"

I remembered Fern reluctantly pulling out the hair wreaths and giving the ladies low buns for the reception, although I could have sworn I saw a couple of the hairdos flash green and red lights later in the evening, but that could have also had something to do with the bride being from the South and that region's fondness for light-up accessories during the holidays. "At least you didn't have to stay until the very end. We were supervising the load out until after two in the morning."

"Another reason why I'm not a wedding planner. Planning Leatrice's wedding was enough for me, thank you very much."

I didn't mention that he'd only partially planned Leatrice's wedding, since I'd secretly gone behind him making sure all the details were in place.

Reese put a small portable speaker from the bedroom on the counter and tapped the screen of his phone. The sounds of holiday music immediately filled the air, and I laughed when I recognized the music from "A Charlie Brown Christmas."

He grinned at me. "It's a classic."

Richard bustled by us again, and I breathed in the savory aroma of the golden brown puffs on the platter he carried. I'd slept as late as I could after my long night, and hadn't had time to eat anything before Richard had arrived to start prepping. I knew better than to try to sneak food past him once he'd started cooking, but I planned to sample the hors d' oeuvres as soon as my hair was deemed ready.

"It's as good as I can do," Fern said, giving my hair one last blast of spray. "I'll just tell everyone we went with a tousled look on purpose."

"There's tousled and there's bed head," Richard said, passing me as he headed back to the kitchen.

Reese grinned at me. "I don't mind bed head."

"I'll bet you don't, big boy." Fern nudged me.

I tried to give him a severe look, but he ignored me, winking at Reese before going to answer the sharp knocking on the door.

"I'm here." Kate burst in as Fern stepped back, her arms filled with wrapped boxes and her bare legs covered with a red skirt so short it reminded me of an ice skating costume.

"Why so many presents?" Fern asked. "I thought we only needed one Secret Santa gift."

Kate jerked her head behind her. "I'm not carrying only mine." She gave me a pointed look, which I knew was because she'd picked up a Secret Santa gift for me on her way in, as well. I held out little hope it wasn't the screaming goat.

Leatrice entered behind her, a deviled egg plate held outstretched in both hands, and Sidney Allen brought up the rear carrying Hermès in a red-and-green plaid blazer. Both wore a red ascot.

I walked over to greet them, glancing down at the plate. "Do those deviled eggs look like little Santas?"

Leatrice beamed at me. "I used pimentos for the hats and mouth, capers for the eyes, and piped cream cheese for the beards and trim."

Richard emerged from the kitchen, both hands on his hips. "What did I say about bringing food?"

"You said not to bring my pigs in blankets wreath," Leatrice said as she walked the plate over to the dining table and wedged it in between two of Richard's platters. "You didn't say anything about deviled egg Santas."

"She has a point," I told Richard, who gave me a murderous look.

Sidney Allen put Hermès on the floor, and the little dog immediately scampered over to Richard, spinning around so that he faced the same way as his master and giving a loud yip.

"At least someone agrees with me," Richard said before turning on his heel and disappearing into the kitchen with Hermès close behind him.

"Don't you two look dashing?" Leatrice said when she'd turned from the table and looked at me and Reese.

"Thank you," my fiancé said. "Not more festive than you, though."

Leatrice giggled and spun in her dress, the giant Santa faces flashing by as the skirt flared. "Aren't you sweet?"

I was grateful she wasn't dressed like Santa again, although I could have done without the red-and-green striped elf hat headband perched on her jet-black hair. At least Sidney Allen was dressed in his usual dark suit, the pants tucked up snug under his chin, and the red ascot his only nod to the holidays.

Kate deposited the wrapped gifts under the tree and headed for the bottles of champagne lined up on the counter between the kitchen and living room. "This calls for a drink."

"What calls for a drink, dear?" Leatrice asked.

Kate began handing out champagne flutes. "Surviving yesterday's wedding, seeing Brianna being hauled off to jail, and finding out what really happened to Kris."

"It was a big night," Leatrice said. "I'm just glad that imposter Santa didn't get away with trying to sabotage your wedding."

"Watching you fly through the air and tackle her might have been one of the greatest moments of my life," Kate said, raising an empty glass to my neighbor. "And her being arrested for stealing our escort card ornaments was a bonus."

"I'll second that," Mack said as he walked in carrying baby Merry on one hip.

Buster followed behind holding a glass vase filled with towering white amaryllis cuffed with a wreath of green holly. "It was almost a shame to pull you off her."

Leatrice blushed, her cheeks reddening beneath her heavy rouge. "That young lady was definitely on the naughty list." She rushed forward to hug Prue. "Unlike other young ladies I know."

"It's shocking to discover that one of the cops who regularly patrolled our neighborhood was actually helping out the criminals," Mack said as he shifted Merry from one hip to the other. "I can't tell you how many times Officer Rogers popped into our shop to say hello."

"I have to take some responsibility for him showing up at the hotel last night," Reese said, holding his glass still as Kate poured champagne into it. "He heard me talking to Annabelle about a Santa being at the Four Seasons, and then he heard me mention his badge number, although at the time it didn't occur to me that was what it was. I had no idea he'd been searching for Kris since his disappearance and that the crime bosses were getting irate that their men were getting nabbed and this vigilante Santa was still on the loose."

"It's not your fault," Leatrice said. "You arrived before any other cops did."

"That's because when I saw Rogers rush out, I got a feeling something was off. I went into his duty roster and saw that he showed up to every crime scene related to Santa. Then I realized that ever since he'd taken the Georgetown beat, crime had been on the rise. He was first on the scene for almost every crime, but there was never any good evidence."

"Because he probably got rid of anything that would implicate the guys paying him off," Kate said.

Leatrice shook her head. "It's sad to see such a young fellow get involved with the wrong crowd."

"He was a part of that crowd before he became a cop," a voice said from the door.

We all turned to face the tall man in the brown suit who stood in the open doorway. It took me a moment to realize it was Kris Kringle Jingle in regular clothes.

"You made it," I said, going to the door and pulling him inside by the elbow. "I invited Kris, Stanley, and Jeannie to celebrate with us."

Kris's friends shuffled in behind him, Stanley looking calmer than he had the night before—now in a blue overcoat instead of a Santa suit —and Jeannie smiling tentatively at Fern, who rushed across the room to hug her and fuss over her hair.

Faces lit up with recognition, and everyone began welcoming the new arrivals.

"Is that why you disappeared?" Fern asked Kris once he'd started working on Jeannie's hair. "You were hiding from a dirty cop?"

"That, and I thought he might have made me," Kris said.

I looked Kris up and down, thinking he cleaned up really well for someone living on the streets. "Made you?"

"I've been working undercover."

CHAPTER 37

L eatrice staggered back a few feet. "You're an undercover agent? For the CIA? The FBI? The DEA?"

Kris chuckled. "I'm actually a confidential informant. Have been for years." He glanced at my fiancé. "Sorry I couldn't let you in on it, Detective."

Reese shook his head. "No worries. I get it. You probably didn't know who to trust. Detectives keep their CIs pretty close to the vest, anyway."

"I've been working with Vice for a while. One of my old service buddies is on the squad and roped me in." Kris rocked back on his heels. "You'd be surprised how a homeless guy dressed as Santa can move around unnoticed."

"How exciting to have one of our employees also work undercover for the police," Mack said, nudging Buster who still looked gobsmacked.

"So you knew Rogers was dirty?" Reese asked.

"I'd seen him running with those same dodgy guys before he went to the academy," Kris said. "I don't think he knew I recognized him from his old life. I doubt he paid attention to a homeless guy when he was making trouble as a teenager. But I spotted him talking with his old crew while he was walking his beat one day. Then there was an uptick in shady things going at night, and the cops never seemed to be around. It didn't take long to realize it was all connected to the larger crime ring in Georgetown we'd been tracking for a while. Rogers was on the take and letting the criminals move drugs and stolen merchandise freely. Problem was, I was pretty sure he saw me when he was talking to his old pals."

"And that's when you tried to stage your own death?" I asked.

He nodded. "I didn't want to blow my cover or end up floating in the Potomac. I asked Stanley to plant the suit, but he was so nervous when Rogers showed up right as he was putting it in the dumpster that he panicked."

Stanley laughed nervously. "He knew I was lying."

"Liars are always good at spotting other liars," Reese said, handing Stanley a glass of champagne.

Kris nodded, rubbing a hand over his gray stubble. "We decided Stanley should disappear too."

"And Jeannie?"

Another nod.

"That explains the cops outside the shelter when we talked to Jeannie," I said. "Were your vice buddies watching her?"

Kris eyed me. "They were supposed to be inconspicuous."

"They were," I assured him, "but Kate's just really good at determining men's professions by their clothes."

Kate winked at him. "The boxy blazers gave them away."

"Where did you all hide?" I asked, looking between the three. "One of the shelters? Fern's storage room?"

Kris gave Fern an apologetic look. "Only a couple of times. We moved around. During the day, we didn't need to hide. We dressed as Santas and rang the bells for Salvation Army."

"Hiding in plain sight," Leatrice said. "Genius."

"And all those criminals who got nabbed?" I asked.

"Part of the larger Vice operation," Kris said, "but the Santa stuff made it seem like an amateur vigilante, so the bad guys didn't know the cops were watching them and closing in."

Reese grinned and nodded. "Not bad."

Carl walked in holding a bottle of bubbly wrapped in a gold

ribbon, a black knit cap covering his close-cropped hair. As soon as I saw him, something clicked, and I pushed my way to the door. "Did you happen to dress up as Santa this week?"

The makeup artist's cheeks flushed. "So you *did* recognize me."

I remembered seeing the Santa in hipster glasses when Kate and I were outside Baked and Wired. "Not at the time, but now that I see you, I realize that's why Santa looked so familiar."

Carl handed me the bottle. "Fern roped me into being one of the Santa stand-ins."

"Of course he did," I said, wondering how many Santas had been roaming the streets of Georgetown under Fern's direction. "Well, I'm glad you're here."

"Don't worry." He gave me a conspiratorial wink and patted his jacket pocket. "I always have emergency stash of bronzer and falsh lashes on me, so we can do something to perk you up before anyone takes photos."

I tried not to take offense at that since I had been up late the night before. "Thanks, Carl."

Kate finished pouring champagne and handed both Carl and Kris a glass. "Let's raise our glasses to Kris Kringle Jingle and his amazing crime-fighting friends."

Loud throat clearing made us all look around at Richard poking his head over the counter from the kitchen and Hermès's tiny furry head right beside his. "Were you going to forget the chef?"

Kate handed him a glass, and we all clinked and drank as the dog yipped merrily.

"You know, dear," Leatrice sidled up to me as everyone began drifting around the room, "maybe we should consider adding Kris to our crime-fighting crew. We could use an experienced CI."

"We don't have a crime-fighting crew," I said, stealing a glance at Reese and seeing the corner of his mouth twitch. "And we don't need our own confidential informant."

Prue held Merry's hands while the girl attempted to toddle over to the brightly decorated Christmas tree, and I hoped not all the ornaments were as fragile as they looked. One glance at the glass coffee table and baubles at the little girl's level reminded me that my place was by no means baby-proof.

"Speaking of crime-fighting crews, Hobbes and your cop buddies are coming, right?" I asked my fiancé.

He polished off his glass and pointed it toward the door. "Here's one of them now, along with…"

I turned to see his brother, Daniel, walk in next to a tall man with sandy-brown hair. "PJ. Don't you remember? Richard's significant other."

Richard waved from the kitchen, splotches of red appearing on his cheeks. Hermès scampered out to greet the handsome man, who scooped him up, fluffed the dog's ascot, and headed for the kitchen.

"I thought you were Richard's significant other," Reese teased.

"I thought *you* were," I shot back.

He laughed, then cocked his head to one side, his brow furrowing as he looked over my head. Kate had run up to Daniel, thrown her arms around his neck, and pulled him into a long kiss.

"Did I miss something?" he asked, pulling his eyes away from his brother to look at me.

I laughed, slipping my hand into his and feeling a rush of warmth that was only partly due to his body heat. "Who knows? It's never dull at Wedding Belles."

"You can say that again."

He gave a weary sigh, and I elbowed him playfully. Before I could remind him how instrumental my crew had been in closing the case on the missing Santa, Kris Kringle Jingle and Leatrice started singing "Hark the Herald Angels Sing" along with the Charlie Brown album. We all joined in, with Merry clapping her hands off beat and Sidney Allen looking pained by the amateur attempt.

As the song wound down, I caught a whiff of perfume that was instantly familiar. I spun toward the door and stared. "Son of a nutcracker."

"I was told there was an engagement party." She smiled widely, her voice rising above the music as everyone turned.

"Is that…?" Reese stared, his voice soft in my ear as my heart hammered away.

I nodded as she dropped her overnight bag on the floor by her feet and touched a hand to her auburn bob, diamonds glittering on her fingers. Swallowing hard, I plastered a smile on my own face.

"It's my mother."

* * *

THANK you for reading CLAUS FOR CELEBRATION!

This book has been edited and proofed, but typos are like little gremlins that like to sneak in when we're not looking. If you spot a typo, please report it to: laura@lauradurham.com
Thank you!!

ALSO BY LAURA DURHAM

Annabelle Archer Series:

Better Off Wed

For Better Or Hearse

Review To A Kill

Death On The Aisle

Night of the Living Wed

Eat, Prey, Love

Groomed For Murder

Wed or Alive

To Love and To Perish

Marry & Bright

The Truffle with Weddings

Irish Aisles are Smiling

Godfather of Bride

Claus for Celebration

Annabelle Archer Books available as Audiobooks:

Better Off Wed

For Better Or Hearse

Dead Ringer

Review to a Kill

Annabelle Archer Collection: Books 1-4

To get notices whenever I release a new book, follow me on BookBub:

https://www.bookbub.com/profile/laura-durham

ABOUT THE AUTHOR

Laura Durham has been writing for as long as she can remember and has been plotting murders since she began planning weddings over twenty years ago in Washington, DC. Her first novel, BETTER OFF WED, won the Agatha Award for Best First Novel.

When she isn't writing or wrangling brides, Laura loves traveling with her family, standup paddling, perfecting the perfect brownie recipe, and reading obsessively.

Find her on:
www.lauradurham.com
laura@lauradurham.com

To get notices whenever she releases a new book, follow her on BookBub:

https://www.bookbub.com/profile/laura-durham

facebook.com/authorlauradurham
twitter.com/reallauradurham
instagram.com/lauradurhamauthor

ACKNOWLEDGMENTS

This book was inspired by "The Compliment Man," who walked around DC in the 90s giving out compliments to everyone he passed. He didn't ask for money, although he was homeless, he just said nice things to brighten people's days as a way to give back to people helping him. I tweaked him and made him into a Santa for this book, but the sentiment is still the same. The world needs more people like "The Compliment Man" and more Santas!

As always, an enormous thank you to all of my wonderful readers, especially my beta readers and my review team. A special shout-out to the beta readers who caught my goofs this time: Patricia Joyner, Linda Reachill, Sheila Kraemer, Linda Fore, Sandra Anderson, Cathy Jaquette, Kaitlyn Platt, Carol Spayde, Christy Kalbhin, Tony Noice, Annemarie Pasquale, Zina Loses. Thank you!!

Big kisses to everyone who leaves reviews. They really make a difference, and I am grateful for every one of them!

Wishing everyone the happiest of holidays!!